Published by Jon Lewis

Copyright © 2024 by Jon Lewis

All rights reserved.

No portion of this book may be reproduced in any form without written permission from the publisher or author, except as permitted by U.S. copyright law.

Cover illustration by Glenn Chadbourne

Contents

Ageless	1
Dedication	2
1. Chapter One	3
2. Chapter Two	22
3. Chapter Three	41
4. Chapter Four	66
5. Chapter Five	90
6. Chapter Six	113
7. Chapter Seven	137
8. Chapter Eight	155
Epilogue	168
Turn the page for a sneak peek at the thrilling sequel to Ageless:	172
Bonus - Chapter One	173
About The Author	177

Ageless

By: Jon Lewis

Dedication

To my best friend and loving wife, Niki.
And my wonderful supportive children, John, Holly, Kate, and Owen.
And to all my friends who have shared in my journey to become an author.
Thank you for being the best part of my life.
Also, a special thanks to my good friend Eric Gabrielsen, whose own journey inspired me to follow this dream myself.

Chapter One

Portland, Maine

"Are you fixing the fence, Henri?" the little girl asked.

"Yes, Maybelline. I am definitely fixing the fence," Henri answered, looking over his shoulder at the little curly-haired girl.

"Daddy said a truck broked'ed it," she said, nodding, her red ringlets bouncing as she walked across the backyard to watch Henri finish pulling off the broken boards with a hammer. He pried each one free and set them on the ground in a small stack.

"It's not too bad, only five broken boards so it is easy to fix. The post is still good." He continued his commentary, explaining what he was doing for his small audience. Maybelline nodded as he spoke; she thought the post looked straight too.

She liked Henri. "He's nice," she told her father later.

Setting up a sawhorse, Henri cut five new boards with a small handsaw and nailed them back into place.

"See? Good as new," he said as Maybelline walked closer to inspect his work and agreed.

"Yup, good as new," she chimed as Henri bent over to start picking up the bits of wood and broken boards.

"I can help, I can help," Maybelline exclaimed, grabbing a broken board.

"Wait!" Henri cried too late, the small nails breaking the skin and scratching her palm as she screamed "Owieeeee! Owieeee!" and pulled her hand away.

"Oh, sweetie, let me see." Henri pulled a handkerchief from his pocket to wrap her hand in. "DAVID! HANNAH!" he shouted from the backyard.

Hannah is the first to the "slider," followed by her husband David. Maybelline stood sobbing as Henri wrapped his handkerchief around her hand.

"MOMMA! OWIE, OWIE!" she screamed as Hannah rushed to her. David saw her bloody hand out the slider and headed back inside to grab a first aid kit.

Hannah scooped up the sobbing girl. "Oh, baby, what did you do? What did you do?"

Henri answered, "She grabbed the board and cut herself on a nail. It does not look too deep, just a scratch."

Through sobs Maybelline stammered, "The board b-b-bited me."

"I'm sorry," Henri said.

"It's okay, you didn't do anything," said Hannah, taking Maybelline inside to take care of the cut. Henri watched them go in before he started picking up the bits of wood. He checked carefully around the grass with a magnet to catch any loose nails, before putting his tools away.

David came out a few minutes later. "How is she?" Henri asked.

"It's okay, just a scratch. Not deep." David handed him back his handkerchief as he looked the work over and then pulled out five twenties.

"You do good work, Henri," he said, handing him the money.

Henri nodded. "Thanks, it was an easy fix and I've been a carpenter for a long time."

Dave looked at him quizzically for a moment. "How old are you?" he asked, studying Henri. Shoulder-length black hair pulled into a tight ponytail. Scruffy beard, dark blue eyes behind his Ray-Bans. If he guessed, he would say early thirties. Henri was not a good-looking man, but he was interesting looking. Deeply tanned and fit from hard labor. His hands and forearms were heavily scarred. Something about his nose and profile made David think of France. The word "Gaul" came to mind. "No, Roman," he thought.

"I will be forty-eight in two months. Why do you ask?" Henri put the bills in his pocket, then carefully folded the handkerchief.

David sputtered for a moment. "Oh? You are in great shape, man. I would have said mid-thirties, thirty-five tops. Thanks for the quick job on the fence. I'll call if I need anything else. I have your number." He turned quickly and walked away, slipping his wallet into his back pocket.

"You are welcome. I hope she is okay," Henri called after him. He put the sawhorse back in Dave's garage and placed the boards in the trash bin. He picked up his small tool bag and saw a blade of grass with three drops of blood on it. He carefully plucked it before walking out front to the curb. After looking both ways, he sucked the blood from the blade of grass. His eyes rolled back in his head for a moment, and he shuddered.

After the ecstatic moment passes, he turned right and walked the three blocks to the bus stop. As soon as he did It, he knew it was a mistake. He just could not help himself. It smelled so good, and it had been so long. It tasted so sweet. Maybelline waved from the window as he walked away, but he didn't see her. By the time he caught the bus, he was sweating profusely.

The Somali bus driver commented, "You look like shit, man, are you okay?"

Henri could barely hear him over the voices whispering to him from the back of his brain. "Je suis tellement stupide" was all he managed to say. It took all his strength not to grab the man by the throat and tear into his neck with his teeth. The lights from the street and headlights blinded him momentarily. He grunted hard and pushed the urges back down. "Je suis tellement stupide," he mumbled again. He gripped his tool bag tightly and found a seat halfway back. Pulling his Ray-Bans over his eyes, he closed them and leaned his head against the cool glass. He held it together until the voices quieted.

The bus driver watched him take a seat, shaking his head, then closing the door and heading for his next stop.

"Hey, Shades."

"Hey, Shaaaaaadeeeeessss," a girl's voice whispered in his ear. Henri opened his eyes; he glanced in the direction of the voice. No one was there. The bus was empty save for a young woman in the back. He hadn't noticed her when he got on, nor had he smelled her either. He did smell patchouli oil, stale cigarettes from the driver, and fried chicken; the sweet smell of Maybelline's blood in his nose, on his breath… The bus reeked of fried chicken.

A bucket was on the floor by the woman's feet. Just bones, each piece chewed and sucked clean of meat and breading. The bus driver stopped at a red light. The brakes hissed. The engine wound down and idled. The girl...no, woman looked up at him briefly from her phones. She had two, one in each hand. Her face was lit in a violet halo of screen light. She was smiling. Her mouth, her features were not symmetrical; a long thin scar split her upper lip, another across her nose horizontally. She had several piercings, eyebrow, lip, and nose. Short brown hair in a pageboy cut. She had sunglasses on too, big garish flowery rims.

They looked at each other for a moment, then the bus jolted as the lights changed. He looked away and closed his eyes again. Even with his shades on, the lights hurt his eyes. After a few minutes he smelled the sea and knew his stop was coming up. He leaned forward and opened his eyes, looking down at the tool bag. Reaching up, he pulled the cord to get off at the next stop. He looked over at the woman, who was looking back and forth between the two phones. The bus stopped and the doors opened with a *whoosh*. He stood up, tool bag in hand. Stepping down onto the curb. A gush of air from the doors closing swirled around him and caught a whiff of something familiar... "Another," he muttered, turning to look at the bus as it pulled away.

As it passed, the woman's face was in the window glancing over at him, mouthing something. "I...see...you." He shook his head to clear it, unsure if what he saw or smelled was even real. He had not met Another in a very long time... The smell was strange, wonderfully feminine and fleeting. Born? or Made? He watched the bus vanish around a corner. He felt flushed and his heart thumped loudly in his chest.

Henri quickly walked in the direction the bus went and took a deep breath; the scent was dissipating rapidly in the breeze. He stopped at the corner and stood there a long time as the sea breeze blew the scent away. He took out his phone and clicked on a contact.

It rang three times. "Hello, Henri, it's been a while."

"Yes, it has," Henri said.

"To what do I owe the pleasure?"

"I am in Portland, Maine. I slipped," Henri confessed.

"Did you kill?" the voice asked.

"No, I didn't," he answered.

There was silence for a few moments then. "You left the Sanctuary?"

"Yes, I needed some supplies and to see other people, if only for a little while," Henri responded.

"I see," the voice said.

"There is Another here. I think Born; the scent is strong but muddled. I would say only newly Born or just recently Made. I only caught the barest whiff of her in passing," Henri explained.

"Hmmm? A She...how interesting... It is forbidden to make Another. For her sake she had better be Born. Though that too might be a complication. I will let the Circle know. Find out who she is, and we will send someone for her," the voice said and hung up.

Henri closed the phone and frowned. She was on the 8 line that made a long run in a rough figure eight route through the city. His RV was parked two blocks away in the park and ride on Back Cove. The 8 crossed back on itself up on Congress Street. He turned and walked briskly toward his RV to drop off his tool bag. If she got off the bus, he would track her scent and find her.

His RV, a refurbished '73 Winnebago, was where he left it. The lot had emptied out; only six vehicles remained. He opened his phone and disabled the security system on the RV. Then he walked around the side and opened the storage door, putting his tools inside. He had a dark blue Henley in there that he pulled over his head, covering the PWT he was wearing. He took a small thermos from his tool bag and drained the dark contents. This settled his stomach and cleared his mind. He reengaged the security system and headed back toward the city.

He looked up at the night sky and the stars twinkling there and sighed. He turned and quickly walked up Franklin, heading toward Monument Square. It was only 9:30 p.m., and lots of people were still on the streets. He headed back to the bus stop and waited for the 8 to come back around. A few minutes later a number 8 came into view, and he recognized the bus driver. Stepping on, he looked down the length of the bus. There were a few people on but not the girl. The chicken smell had abated; her scent was faint but present.

"Sorry," he said, stepping back out the door.

The driver gave him a weird look and muttered, "Whatever." The girl had gotten off on the Mercy Hospital/Maine Medical Center loop. He backtracked the route around the city, heading up Congress Street toward Maine Med. The large hospital shone like a beacon; so many bright lights hurt his eyes. He looked down as he walked toward it.

Passing Maine Med, he continued until he came around past Mercy Hospital. He was almost back to Monument Square when he picked up her scent again. She had gotten off a block from the square. He swore to himself as he realized he had walked the long way around.

Still, he had her scent now. She had walked down Danforth toward the waterfront. He tracked her to a garbage can; the chicken bucket was there. She had vomited into the trash bin; the smell was very strong, and he wrinkled his nose. There was some splatter beside the can on the ground as well. He followed what was left of her scent still hanging in the air.

Picking up his pace, he turned down Commercial Street. There was some light traffic and several people on the street. He had walked along the waterfront almost all the way to the end where the road turned up Franklin. Her scent was growing stronger.

As he approached the Royal Garden Hotel, he saw her. Just inside talking to the front-desk manager, who handed her a small paper bag. She thanked the man and walked toward the elevators.

Looking down at his watch he noted it was now 10:30 p.m. He waited and watched. A short time later a light came on in the front corner room on the fourth floor that overlooked the harbor. The lights went back out almost immediately. Then the curtains opened wider, and a single silhouette stood in the window. He took off his shades and could see her much more clearly; his night vision was very acute. She was sipping from a pink bottle of Antiacid. She turned her head and looked directly at him for a few moments, then moved away from the window.

Portland, Maine

"Every night it's the same, the paranoia that someone is watching me, following me," I thought to myself. Tonight was no different. The room lights hurt my eyes as soon as I turned them on. And I could feel another migraine coming on, so I just turned them off again. I didn't know what was wrong with me, so I went to the window to look out at the city and Portland Harbor. They were a beautiful sight at night. The moon and lights sparkling on the water were so bright.

Suddenly I felt the hair on my arms and neck stand on end, as if someone was watching me. Then I noticed a man on the street looking up at me. I could see him so clearly in the moonlight. The man from the bus, his arms crossed and smiling up at me. He was holding his sunglasses in his hand. He had changed his shirt too.

God, he had smelled so good on the bus. I had wanted to ask what cologne he was wearing but he fell asleep too quickly. And before I could get another chance, I started feeling sick from eating that entire bucket of chicken. So, I just looked back at my parents' phones at all the pictures we took over the years. I miss them both so much.

As I looked at the man, I could feel the anxiety returning. Rising and falling like waves lapping against the shore of my mind. Trying to wear me down and wash me away or drown me.

I sipped the rest of the antiacid and stepped back from the window, shaking my head, trying to clear it. I threw the empty bottle at the trash can and missed. Then went and checked the door again for the fifth time to make sure it was locked. *Click click. Click click*, just to be sure.

Returning to the window I could see the man was gone.

"Was he even there in the first place?" I asked myself, shaking my head again. I tried to slow down my breathing and tried to push the anxiety back down. As I was doing this, I noticed how bad my shoes smelled, so I sat down on the bed and removed them. Then

I took the pair into the bathroom and started rinsing each one off in the sink.

More strong smells assailed my nose. "Ugg, I stink," I said, catching a whiff of myself. The smells seemed to intensify in waves. In a panic I smelled my hands and armpits and grimaced. Everything smelled *bad bad bad*. The toilet and sink drain smelled awful too. I could smell my own crotch through my pants. Every smell seemed magnified and overwhelming. I started sobbing uncontrollably. "What's wrong with me?" I cried, shaking as I peeled my disgusting-smelling clothing off and stepped into the shower.

I turned the tap to the hottest setting and pulled the handle up before it even got hot warm. I just stood sobbing and shaking until the water ran from cold to hot, then turned it down to a tolerable level. The water helped. The steam helped. But, god, the bathroom light was too bright, so I reached out and flicked it off. I turned on the Rain setting and sat in the tub with the water flowing down over me. I put my head in my hands, closed my eyes, and waited for the panic to subside. It took a very long time.

After midnight I finally exited the shower. The mirrors and walls were heavy with condensation.

"Damn, I forgot to turn the exhaust fan on." As I flicked it on, I felt a sharp pain in my gut, a strong pang of hunger. "Again?"

I tore through my bag on the counter and found a protein bar, chewed it down before taking my nighttime meds. After I brushed my teeth, I wiped the mirror with a towel and looked at myself in the glass. Most people couldn't see the scars; the plastic surgeon had done a decent job of hiding the four horizontal slash marks across my face. But I could see them.

Running my finger over the one that split my lip, I could feel the rubbery scar tissue beneath. I frowned and tried to hold my face in a more neutral position. The scars were almost invisible when I did that. But if I smile or laugh or talk, the skin puckers along the lines. Then everyone stares at me, trying to guess who cut up my face.

"I'm just going crazy, aren't I?" I said to myself.

"Yup, and crazy tired too." After I dried off, I climbed into bed nude. I could not be bothered with underwear. I felt better almost immediately as my legs slid across the cool sheets. My sleep meds kicked in pretty fast, and I sighed, pulling the covers up over my shoulders and falling asleep quickly.

The dreams came shortly afterward. Always the same. My first patrol in-country, escorting some friendlies back to their village. The rugged mountains were breathtaking, the thin air cool and crisp.

"El Te" on my six talking into the radio, "Larry" and "Moe" at eleven and two o'clock. I had a habit of giving everyone a special nickname. They were always funny and fit the person well, and they usually stuck once others heard me use them. At least that's how it was during basic and follow-on training. My guys did not seem to mind so they let me do it.

We had passed this way an hour earlier and the drones had swept the length of the valley for vehicles and movement thirty minutes ago. We saw a boy herding goats toward the mud houses along the dirt track and their pen. He was a cutie, with long dark hair and soulful eyes. His face was dirty and dusty, and he looked so tired. There were two little girls standing in a doorway looking at me. Their mother was kneeling behind them and had an arm across each one. All three stared at us as we passed and then Mom pulled them inside into the dark room beyond.

It was getting dark but only two kilometers left to the FOB. It got dark quickly on the leeward side of the mountain as the sun set behind it. You could see the darkness sweeping ominously across the valley below through the spare gnarled pines.

Something heavy suddenly hit me from above. Driving me down to the ground. I can hear myself scream as I feel a sharp pain between my neck and shoulders. I felt a collarbone crack as it gave out too. A branch raked across my face; blood ran into my eyes, blinding me.

"El Te" was shouting something but his voice was drowned out by automatic weapon fire. I blacked out for a moment and felt myself being dragged. I hurt so bad and tried to struggle but couldn't clear my head or see clearly. Everything was fuzzy and gray. There was a lot of shouting. I could hear a woman wailing, children screaming. Then everything went black again.

As I started coming to, the first thing I noticed was the smell. The stink of blood, shit, and urine. I still could not see clearly; my vision was still so blurry. There was grunting and movement across the room. I could hear cloth being torn somewhere.

Finally, one eye cleared enough to see, and I caught sight of two men, dressed the same as the locals. They were dirty and wearing loose-fitting clothes. There were dead bodies in a heap on the floor: the woman, the two girls, the boy, my guys…two other men who looked like the guys standing across from me. God, I wanted to scream but held it in. Everyone had been slashed up and torn apart. The two men were tearing clothes from one of the little girls, lapping up the blood from her wounds as they did so. I started feeling around with my hand toward my belt webbing and fingered the safety off my sidearm.

Somehow, they heard me moving and their heads turned quickly to look at me. Their eyes in the lantern light glowed like those of a feral animal, like coyotes. They made me think of coyotes. I managed to slide my gun free as they turned to leap at me screeching. Blood spewing from their mouths, their teeth sharp and pointy. Their gloved hands had razors sewn into them along each finger. Lantern light reflected off the blades as they leaped.

They leaped as I screamed and fired. I got the one on the right in the neck through and through and then the left one in the chest. Their hands outstretched, clawing for me. They landed on top of me as I squeezed off another round, hitting one in the chin and blowing his jaw apart. I could feel their hands clawing at my wrist, trying to get control of the gun. My wrist burned where the blades cut into it. The screeching turned into a moan that stopped abruptly. The one with his jaw gone, tongue bobbing and dangling down, flailed on top of me. He twitched a bit and was finally still.

I let go of the gun and struggled to push them both off me but the pain between my shoulders was too much. My arms were so heavy. There was blood and bits of crunchy bone and tissue in my mouth. My face was covered in a mask of gore. I was drowning in it. Struggling and sinking down into darkness, drowning in blood and gore, I started to scream.

I woke up in the hotel room screaming. Tearing the blankets away as sweat poured off me in sheets. It did not take long before someone was banging on the door. "ARE YOU OKAY?!" a man called out.

"Is she okay?" a woman could be heard asking behind him.

The phone rang at the same time. I was shaking so hard as I picked it up, I missed part of what was said. But it was the front desk asking if I was okay as well; someone had reported screaming.

"I'm sorry, I'm so sorry. I have PTSD. I'm so sorry, it was just bad dreams," I told them.

The man banged on the door again. "Are you sure you're, okay? I'm a cop. Is anyone harming or threatening you?"

"No!" I went to the door and answered, my throat ragged and sore from screaming. "I am fine, really. I'm a vet with bad PTSD. It was just a dream...just a dream."

"Okay, okay, I'm a vet too. I get it. If you need someone to talk to or to sit with you for a bit, my wife and I are right next door. It is no problem," he said.

"No, I am okay now. I am okay. Thank you. I am so sorry."

After they left, I walked over to the bed and remade it. I pulled the covers up and put the pillows on top. The clock said 5:23 a.m.

"I'm never getting back to sleep." I sighed and walked over to look at the hotel-provided coffee maker, then eyed the house brand packets of coffee skeptically and grimaced. "Ugh."

Opening my phone, I did a quick search and found a Starbucks three blocks away that opened at 6:00 a.m. "Okay, I guess I'm up and going for a walk."

***

Henri watched as she crossed the lobby with long strides toward him. Lauren pushed the door open and stepped outside. She froze for a moment.

"The man."

"The man from the bus."

"The man from the window was just standing there. Leaning against the wall of the building next door. Reading a book...in the dark," I thought. He just stood there leaning against the wall smiling at me. "Are you—are you following me?" I hissed as a knot in my stomach started to grow, adrenaline kicking in as I prepared for fight-or-flight. He was a big guy, not tall but wide with huge arms.

"Yes. I am," he answered calmly, closing the paperback.

I did not expect him to say yes. I blinked several times.

"What do you want?" I asked quickly, glancing over my shoulder. We were in full view of the front desk.

Then I caught a whiff of him... He smelled so good. Like nothing I had ever smelled before. It was like the very essence of what a man should smell like, distilled and enhanced to a mouthwatering level.

"My name is Henri," he said. His accent was interesting.

"He is definitely French," I thought.

"I would like to get a cup of coffee with you and perhaps talk," he said calmly and sincerely.

"I—I was going to get coffee now. How do I know you're not some serial killer stalking young women? I am an army vet; I could kick your ass," I said tersely.

"Ah," he said, nodding. "I too have been to war, but it was a long time ago. I would make a poor serial killer." He shook his head in the negative. "I have been standing out here all night, in full view of at least three security cameras. The police stopped forty-six minutes ago to ask me what I was doing and checked my ID. They have my name. I assure you; I have no ill intentions toward you. I simply want to get a coffee and talk to you."

I really was not sure what to say but... "Fuck, he is strangely charming," I thought to myself. "And he smells so good," I thought, again.

The animal part of my brain wanted me to bury my face in his hair and take a deep breath. And maybe...lick sweat off his chest and then undo his belt... I coughed and tamped the carnal urges down hard.

"What's wrong with you?" I asked myself.

"Okay...I guess," I finally answered him, a little flustered. "I, uh, was walking to Starbucks if you want to come along."

"Wonderful." He smiled and noticed me suddenly blushing.

He waited for me to walk past, then walked beside me. "As I said, I am Henri. And you are?"

"Oh, I'm Lauren." I let out a nervous laugh.

"Ah, Lauren."

I really liked how he said it; his accent was very, very French. "Loh-ren..."

"What did you want to talk about?"

"Let us get the coffee and walk a bit first if you do not mind? Then we will talk," he answered, smiling. I shrugged.

We walked the three blocks in silence as the city started to awaken and arrived as Starbucks opened. It felt oddly calming to walk with him. We both ordered coffee. He paid with a twenty-dollar bill and left the rest as a tip. Then we stepped back outside.

I took a long sniff of my coffee before taking a sip. It smelled wonderful, the scent was so strong and earthy. I let out a very long and satisfying "Mmmmmm…"

"Have you noticed recently that what you smell seems much more…powerful…more potent? Those little smells you barely noticed before are now…very strong?" he asked before taking a sip of his drink.

I was flustered but said, "Uh…yes. I, uh, thought I might be pregnant, and it was maybe morning sickness. But the test was negative."

"Have you had any sensitivity to light? I noticed you were wearing sunglasses on the bus," he said.

"Yes, and so were you," I shot back.

"Yes, I was."

"And you were reading a book in the dark," I pointed out.

"Yes, I was," he said again, nodding.

"Were you really reading it, though?" I asked skeptically.

"Yes, I'll show you." He nodded, pointing to the alley. "There," he said, stepping into the deepest shadow of the alleyway and reading aloud a passage from the book he was carrying.

"How are you doing that?" I asked.

"The same way you can. Just like how clearly you saw me last night from the window." He offered me the book.

"What do you mean? Let me see that." He stepped back into the light, handing me the book. The sun was not rising yet and it didn't seem very dark to me, but I moved into the deep shadow, opened the book midway, and looked at the pages. The words were visible but the more I concentrated the clearer they became. Like wearing high-def night vision goggles.

"How? What?" Then I recalled how clearly I could see him from so far away on the darkened street before.

"You've been smelling things, having headaches, eyes getting more and more sensitive to light," he summarized.

"For a while now, the migraines have been terrible." I nodded.

"Unexplainable hunger pangs. Things you loved before not tasting right, not tasting good…not satisfying your hunger," he said as if he knew this already.

"How do you…how do you know that? I haven't even told my doctor all this yet," I stammered.

"It has happened to me too," he said. "Your body is trying to tell you something. It is trying to tell you that it needs something, that it *wants something*." He sipped his coffee as I stepped back out of the shadow still clutching the book.

"What does it want?" I asked.

"This." He took a small flask from his back pocket, opened it, swirled it around a little, and took a sip. Then he offered it to me.

I caught a whiff, and it smelled fantastic. I breathed in deeply. Whatever it was, I knew I needed it right now. The entire world just went away. All I wanted was what was in that flask. I dropped the book and coffee, splattering the liquid over my feet. I did not know what it was, but I knew at that moment that I would kill him if he kept it from me. I stalked toward him as I bared my teeth. I was prepared to tear him limb from limb if he didn't share.

The animal part of my brain roared. Tearing the flask from his hand, I heard myself growling and gulped down a swig. It was salty and pulpy, and there was a minty, oniony, it had mutton flavor; something coppery too, and— "Oh my god, good."

Time seemed to slow down as I savored the taste. Then I tilted the flask back and drank it all, licked as far inside as my tongue would go. I felt a little dribble down my chin and wiped it away, sucking my fingers clean. I even snatched the screwcap from his hand and licked that clean.

"More, I NEED more." I could feel how deep my voice was. Like a powerfully sexual and demanding request.

"I have no more here. But if you come with me, I can give you more. I can give you all that you could ever want or need," he said. "And I can tell you what is happening to you."

The rest was a blur. Rushing back to the hotel to get my bags and check out. A brisk walk through the city. The sun, warm on our backs, rising behind us. Climbing into his RV, him opening the fridge door and that smell. That smell pouring out of it. He gave me bottle after bottle of the thick red liquid.

"What is it?" I asked as I eagerly gulped it down.

"The blood of goats and sheep," he answered, and I did not care. I just drank and drank until I could drink no more. Then I grew so weary. I could not keep my eyes open and sunk back into the couch. All the anxiety, the hunger pains went away. I drifted off to sleep and felt him put a blanket over me. I was warm and so comfortable. I slept the sleep of the dead.

Chapter Two

Gilead, Maine

I awoke with a start, a line of drool at the corner of my mouth. I reached up and wiped it away. Sitting up I realized I was on the couch in Henri's RV. My shoes were off on the floor beside it. It was sunny outside, but the windows were heavily tinted, filtering just enough light that it wasn't painful to look at. "Hello?" I called, but no one answered. I was alone.

I started noticing the smells: blood in the empty bottles in the sink, Henri's scent, manure, pine trees too. I felt around for my phone. It was still in my pocket. I clicked it on and checked to see if I had cell service, two bars. It was 2:34 p.m. Clicking on Maps and turning on Location Services. A dot centered on Gilead, Maine, at the far end of Old Gammon Road. I was in western Maine, about two hours northwest of Portland. I clicked on aerial views, forest, and mountains. Zooming in I could see seven buildings in a circular cluster, fields to the east. The Androscoggin River was nearby, to the north. I closed the phone and slipped my shoes on. My bag was in the chair across from the couch, my luggage beside it.

I suddenly had to pee. I found the bathroom, relieved myself, and washed my hands. Then I checked the door; it wasn't locked and opened easily.

The smell of goats and sheep and manure was heavy in the air. I could see chickens scratching in the dirt. The sunlight hurt my eyes, so I slipped my flower sunglasses back on. Looking around there were sheep and goats in a field nearby, a huge vegetable garden as well. Six large barns and a huge log chalet with dark windows. A small swirl of smoke was coming from the chimney. The RV was parked in front of a barn whose big door was propped open with a pitchfork. I looked inside and saw a green Land Rover, a red pickup as well—a very old Chevy. There were a couple of dirt bikes, and a small red tractor. Beyond them it looked like there was a well-appointed shop that included a lift.

I turned toward the house and noticed a medium-sized black Lab lying in the sun, panting in the grass and looking at me. I swear he was smiling at me.

"Well, hello there," I said, as he got up and trotted over to me, tail wagging. I let him smell my legs, then my hand. He licked it twice and sat down looking up at me expectantly. I scratched behind his left ear, and he leaned into it.

"Oh, you like that, don't you? Where is Henri?" I asked, scratching under his chin next.

The dog stood back up and padded toward the house, tail wagging. I followed along after him, looking around the dooryard in the too bright afternoon light. Then I suddenly realized for the first time in a long time that I felt fine. Other than the sunlight being too bright. I felt "normal" again. It had been so long since I felt this way, I practically skipped up the steps of the broad wide porch.

The dog nosed the front door open; it had not been closed all the way. I could hear music and a man singing. Henri was in the kitchen beyond the living room cooking. A bottle of wine was open, and a single half-full glass sat nearby. He was in a dark T-shirt and jeans, and his long dark hair was pulled into a loose man bun. I had never really liked that look for men, but it suited him. He really was not bad looking, a bit rough and very buff. It looked like his nose had been broken several times and his arms were covered in horrible scars.

Henri's singing voice was surprisingly good. I joined in, singing the next part: "Put your hands on me. I need a little give-and-take." He looked up and smiled at me. He raised a hand in hello. I kept singing the rest as I crossed the room.

***

The chalet was huge on the inside, vaulted all the way up three stories high. A large living room with leather seating and windows to the ceiling. A nice fireplace with stacked stone surrounding it.

"You have a good voice," he commented, tapping his phone and turning the music down. "You look better. How do you feel?" He shoved a long skewer through chunks of meat.

"I feel normal again. Thank you. I cannot remember when I last felt normal. I have been sick for so long."

He nodded. "What you are going through is rough. I had no one to help me when it happened to me." His smile slipped away, his face darkening briefly. He reached over and took a sip of wine. Then he put the kebab on the rack in front of him and shook some spices over it. They were very exotic smelling and aromatic.

"So...you said you were going to tell me what this is. What is going on?" I asked in a more serious tone.

"Yes, about that." He frowned. "You may want to sit down; this may take a little while." He offered me a glass of wine.

I put up my hand. "No thank you." It smelled wonderful, though.

"Henri, please just tell me," I said, sitting down opposite him at the island.

He wiped his hands on a towel as he spoke. "Very well. Please understand something. First, no matter what you have heard or may think, magic is not real. The myths and legends we grow up hearing are not real. But some do have foundations in the truth."

"Okay," I said.

"Why is he talking about magic?" I thought to myself.

"There is no easy way to say this... You and I are what the myths regarding vampires are based upon." He seemed completely sincere and appeared in deep pain telling me this. I wasn't sure how to react. But he continued with what he needed to tell me.

"You and I are humans. The same as everyone. But we have a genetic anomaly that the rest of humanity does not have."

I nodded in response. "Go on."

"Normally humans have six types of stem cells in their bodies, which live in the long bones in our marrow. They perform many functions, from growing blood cells to replacing damaged tissue. I am not a doctor, so my technical understanding is limited. But you and I have a seventh stem cell, a rare thing that when we reach a certain age, usually in our late teens or early twenties, becomes active. This seventh cell supercharges the rest of the other stem cells, and they become overactive. Some of the side effects of this reaction cause useful changes like enhancing our senses, our supersensitive sense of smell and the ability to see very well even in near total darkness. We heal faster and recover from injuries quicker. What might take a week for most humans would only take a few days for us."

He put the towel down. "There are some downsides. The sensitivity to light, for example. The debilitating headaches and hunger pangs if we do not consume blood regularly. This overcharging of the cells means our bodies need fuel. We need to consume the components the stem cells need to work, to function, and those components are found in the blood and marrow of other warm-blooded animals like goats and sheep," he said, then took a sip of wine.

"They need to be consumed in raw form, cooking ruins them and we don't get the full effect."

"So? We are vampires," I surmised.

He looked at me with a pained expression and nodded. "Yes, in a way, yes. We need to drink blood and are better suited to being active at night because of the light sensitivity. Though we do not use that term.

"We call ourselves the Curvel, the People of the Night. But we are not magical, we are not evil undead monsters who sleep in coffins or burn in the sunlight." He sat down and continued.

"I was a Catholic for most of my life and I have never once burst into flames entering a church or taking Holy Sacrament."

"Okay." I was still skeptical but at the same time, it made sense. Drinking the blood had restored me and made me feel whole again.

"What else? That can't be it?" I said.

He leaned forward, his hand flat on the island top. "We can die the same as and in the same way as any other human from disease, accidents, a plate of bad clams. But we also have very, very long-life spans."

I could feel his discomfort. It was clear he thought I might not believe him. "How long is *very*? How long can we live? How many of us are there?"

He leaned back again and finished his wine. "Well, first it is important to know that there are two types of people like us. Those who were Born this way and those of us who were Made this way. We can tell the difference by how we smell. I was Made a Curvel. As was my friend Rami. But you…you smell like you were Born this way and somehow Made this way at the same time. I have never met any of our kind that smelled like that." He poured some more wine and took a long sip.

He went on. "We are one in one hundred million, so very few of us exist. Those of us who were Made age quite slowly. I have aged maybe one year for every ten that I have lived since I was Made. I was born in 1672. Those who were Born can live even longer. No one has been able to measure how long precisely. But there are legends of such people who are seemingly immortal throughout human history. War, famine, disease, something always happens. We all die eventually."

"And Rami, he is one of us too?" I said.

"Yes, he was Made like me. He is on his way; I expect him later today. I am making his favorite dish. He loves my goat," Henri said.

"So, 1672? Where?" I asked.

He nodded and continued, "I was born in a village named Etretat, on the channel coast of France. Near the Port City of Le Havre."

"And you were Made? How does that happen? Being Made, do you just bite someone on the neck or...?"

"No, no, no." He put up a hand. "You must transfer your stem cells, your blood, from one person to another. Wound to wound. It is not an easy thing to do. I was in an accident. Rami was too. A broken bone dripping blood and marrow into an open wound was typically how it happened in the olden days." He looked down at the scars on his arms.

I gasped. My mind flashed back to Afghanistan. To the ambush. The hut. The fiends who attacked us. To all the blood and gore. The horror of it all, knowing their blood had run into my mouth, my eyes, seeping into my wounds, poisoning me.

I felt an episode coming on. The anxiety began to wash over me in waves.

The dog started to whine. His ears flattened and his tail dropped between his legs. He barked once and ran out the open front door.

I could feel myself shaking. My lips were numb, and everything went gray. Henri rushed around and put his hand on my shoulder. But I slapped it away and pushed the stool back so hard it fell over. Henri caught it as I rushed to the sink to retch and vomit. I could sense Henri moving next to me again. I put my hand up, warning him away from me. He stood there holding a hand towel if I needed it.

I slid down onto the floor and curled up into a ball. My eyes were clenched shut as I sobbed. I could feel him sit down next to me, his hand tentatively touching my shoulder. I did not push it away this time. I lay there a long time, and he sat stroking my back until I regained my composure. Finally, I turned to him bleary eyed and said, "I think I'm hungry for normal food. What's for lunch?"

He smiled and said, "I have some fresh tuna salad made. I will make us some nice sandwiches, and could I interest you in a Bloody Mary? It is the house specialty." He got up.

I sat up beside him and said, "That would be nice."

He pulled me up. "God, he smells so good," I thought.

Henri made sandwiches and two delicious, very bloody Bloody Marys, with goat's blood, tomato juice, spices, Worcestershire sauce, and celery. We ate mostly in silence, at the island. Though I did *num num* a few times. The bread he had made was fantastic.

The kitchen was huge, the stove a Viking model. It was set up like a restaurant kitchen, all stainless steel. Even a walk-in fridge and freezer. He put the goat kebabs into the fridge for tonight, then washed and dried his hands and said, "I am a little tired. I have been up for thirty hours. I may take a nap." He began clearing the dishes.

"Oh, of course you must be exhausted," I said, helping load the dishwasher before we headed upstairs.

"I have ten bedrooms, each with its own private bath on the second and third floors. They are all currently empty. You can pick one if you like. If you wish to stay here until you figure out what you want to do next."

"Oh god, I hadn't even considered what I wanted to do next. I thought about moving to Maine. It is so safe and quiet here. I had family up North, but they've all passed away. I was going to start looking for an apartment in Augusta; I wanted to be near Togus VA, where I get my care. If I can stay here until I get my bearings, that would be great," I said.

"You can stay as long as you like. As long as you need to. I built the compound so that our kind had a place to stay while they reestablish themselves. I have not had anyone here for some time. Though my friend Rami comes to visit a couple times a year."

"Reestablish themselves?" I asked, a little confused.

"When you do not age and the people around you do, they start to notice. They start to ask questions," he explained, shrugging as we climbed the stairs.

"When I lived in France, Canada, and southern Maine, I would only stay in one place for no more than ten years and move on. Become someone else if I needed to. I got tired of that. I wanted to have a place of my own, someplace I could build and love and not have to leave." He pointed to the first room. "This one is mine. Rami likes that one there, and the rest are free."

I looked and nodded. "Okay, thanks. I'll have a look and see. I feel good right now. I wanted to go for a run. Is there a trail nearby?"

He nodded and gestured with his hands to the right out the front door.

"Yes, there is. It starts behind the barn with the cars in it. You cannot miss it. I run it regularly and keep it clear; it goes north up to the river, then east around the fields where the sheep graze. You can either follow the field around or take the left fork, which runs out to the road just below the gate to this property. Then back down the road to the house. It is about a mile and a half in total. All right, I will see you in a little while." He went into his room and closed the door.

***

I wandered around the house. It was huge. Each room was nicely appointed. Big comfortable beds and nice furniture. Bookshelves lined with books, so many books. Many in English and French, a few in Arabic, German, and...Welsh? The rooms all had a masculine feel to them, though; there wasn't much about any that had a feminine hand in decorating. One room on the third floor had a big soaker tub with jets, so I chose that one before going back to the RV to get the rest of my things. Then I laid out my toiletries, put my clothes away, and changed into shorts, a T-shirt, and sneakers.

Outside I found the trail head right where he said it was. The dog came padding up to me, tail wagging. I scratched his chin and said, "Well, hello, handsome. I forgot to ask your name."

He licked my hand, and I took off for my run. It felt so good to be able to exercise like this.

My arms and legs warmed up quickly as I ran through the forest. All sorts of new smells assailed me, though. The thick, mucky smell of fungus in the rotting vegetation, squirrels bounding here and there. I caught whiffs of them when they crossed my path. They smelled bitter, like how acorns taste if you chew on them. The trail itself was well traveled, clear and wide. Trip hazards like roots and stones had been removed so I was able to maintain my speed. I smelled the river ahead well before it came into view.

There were lots of ferns near the shore. I've heard they can be harvested in the spring. Fiddleheads were supposed to taste good but were poisonous if eaten raw.

The Androscoggin was wide and deep, the banks high and precipitous. The trail ran along the banks for a quarter mile. I saw a group of kayakers paddling downstream and waved; a few raised their paddles in response.

The trail turned sharply inland. I checked my pulse; it was good, and I felt great. I could smell the fields ahead in the breeze as I ran: goldenrod, tall tassel-topped grasses, sweet honeysuckle, dung from the sheep and goats. I ended up doing two laps before stopping to rest.

As I cooled down, I checked out the barns. They were all unlocked. One was for the animals, full of stalls, feed, and hay. Another had a blacksmith's forge with some ancient-looking tools alongside a power hammer, grinders, and storage for metal stock. Another was a nice woodworking shop, with lathes and table saws and old-looking planers and some tools I had never seen before. A huge, ornate set of bookshelves nearly finished; intricate carvings lined the edges—trees and vines, birds, a fish. Long thin pieces were in clamps on a large worktable, the raw stock already marked ready to carve.

There was a barn for storage of all kinds of things: old car parts, a horse-drawn buggy. The last one wasn't finished. Its exterior walls and cladding were up, and the main beams and supports were in place, but there was no flooring for the upper levels. There was a portable mill, raw lumber that I assumed was drying out after being cut and milled.

I continued to cool down and walked a few more turns around the circular driveway. The dog followed me at first, then sat in the shade of the porch, watching me pant in the heat. I was about to go in and have a shower when a car pulled into the drive.

A nice dark gray Tesla with tinted windows slowly parked in front of the house. The driver's-side door opened and out came a smiling middle-aged man who appeared to be of Middle Eastern descent. Dark, happy eyes and swarthy skin.

***

I walked toward him as he spoke. "Good day, miss, would you be Lauren?"

"Yes, I am. Are you Rami?"

"Yes, yes I am. Henri did tell you I was coming then," he said.

"He did, and also that you were close friends," I answered, smiling.

"Wonderful." He stepped closer and offered his hand. "It is such a pleasure to meet you."

I took his hand as he said, "If I may?" and brought my hand up to his face, smelling my palm for a long time; then he sniffed the back of my hand before returning to my palm again. It was a sweet, intimate feeling.

The breeze shifted and I suddenly caught his scent now too, very much like Henri's but with a few subtle differences. He smelled as delicious as Henri. It was intoxicating. I felt myself blush and a deep thrill ran through my core. My heart skipped several beats. It was disconcerting to feel this level of attraction to both these men. These strangers.

"Do you all smell this good? Do I smell good to you?" I asked.

"Oh yes. Your smell is most invigorating, but our scent is only perceptible and stimulating to our own kind. Only we have the nose for it. I imagine Henri has had to keep a tight rein on his libido. He is French, you know. I am sure he has imagined all sorts of very provocative things since he met you." He nodded, laughing jokingly. But I did not really think he was.

"Henri was right, you are Born and there is a hint of a Maker spoor as well, subtle but distinct, nonetheless. A true rarity you are. One of a kind, such a wonderful surprise."

He finally released my hand. "Shall we go inside? I can bring my things in later."

Just then, the dog came padding up.

"Napoleon! What a good boy!" he cried, rubbing the dog's head.

"Henri is upstairs napping. I was just going to shower and change," I told him.

"Oh, very good, by all means go shower. I will bring my things in then and settle in. I am very thirsty and need a drink of water, and then I am looking forward to Henri's special blend with dinner."

"Okay, I'm sure he will be up soon. I'll be down in a bit." I headed upstairs.

After I showered and changed, I went back downstairs. I could hear the two men speaking in French and laughing. From his tone, it sounded like Rami was teasing Henri about something. But my French is poor, having taken only a single semester when I was sixteen, which I am now regretting.

***

They were sitting close together on the big couch. Napoleon was getting a good scratching from Rami. His tongue lolled lazily out of the corner of his mouth. You could see how close the two men were; their eyes sparkled when they laughed. They seemed to be more like brothers. When they saw me, they switched back to speaking English. Rami spoke first.

"We were just talking about you, Lauren. Do you like goat meat? Henri makes the best goat kebab, better than even my mother's."

Henri laughed. "That's not saying much. You told me your mother was a terrible cook, so I can never be sure if it's really any good." We all laughed.

Another bottle of wine was opened and a glass was poured for me. This time I had some. The fragrance was so interesting, delicate and complex. I finally began to understand what the wine snobs I knew were always talking about.

Rami grew serious for a moment. "Lauren will have to be the judge, then. You will see, Lauren. It is the best you have ever had."

"I have only had goat meat a few times, in Afghanistan, from street vendors. I like it better than lamb," I said. "Mmm...this wine is very good. How long have you two been friends?" I asked.

They looked at each other, then Rami spoke. "That is a very long story, and it would require many more bottles of wine to tell it fully."

He leaned forward and put his hands together. "There are things I need to tell you and make you aware of first. It is why I am here. I needed to witness that Another had been found and verify that you were indeed Born. I am Rami Alcide an emissary for the Circle. The Circle is a group of Born who we consider our leaders. They are like a government. They set rules that we, all Born and

Made, agree to follow. They protect the secrecy of our existence from the outside world."

"Okay..." I wasn't sure where this was going.

"There are only a few rules, but they are absolute. No more can be Made unless the Circle has been petitioned and agreed. To do so against the Circle's wishes is a death sentence for both. There is a caveat for those Made accidentally. This is a recent change, though. An unknown Born in transition donated blood and inadvertently created a Made. They have now both joined us," he added. "We may not hunt, kill, or feed off our human brothers and sisters. Once we start seeing our brothers and sisters as prey, we lose the right to call ourselves human and our lives are forfeited. Anytime you meet a new Born or Made that is unknown to you, you must report it to me. I will give you a number to call or text." He raised a finger to punctuate the air as he explained.

"I am the current emissary for North America to the Circle. If you live long enough and prove yourself worthy, you as a Born may find a seat on the Circle in a few hundred years, at the earliest." He looked to see if I understood. I nodded but said nothing.

He went on. "Until then, all non-seated Born and the remaining Made make up what we call the Ring. If you need help, a new identity. A safe place to be, you contact me. If it is within my power and resources to arrange, I will arrange it for you. My office is in Washington, DC. You need not pay for this service. We who have lived so long have gathered the influence and resources to cover nearly any need or situation. We love and care for our brothers and sisters and will truly try to help you if we can." He looked again to see if I understood or had questions. I honestly did not, as it didn't seem like I had a choice in joining this "club."

"I am required to make a report of this discussion with Henri as a witness and I am also required to request a life/medical history. You may refuse that part if you wish, though. But the more information the Circle has the better. They will be extremely interested to know more about the Maker's spoor I detect in your scent. They may want a sample of your bone marrow to run genetic testing. If someone is Making others, they will want to put an end to that."

"I...I will have to think about that," I said, answering the question about the marrow testing. "I will share my history but only if you agree to share yours. I would like to know more about each of you. How, or why, you were Made and what you have been up to since then." I bit my lip, not sure if I was asking for too much.

"I don't need to know everything. But it would make me more comfortable sharing my own story."

Henri suddenly seemed uncomfortable; he fidgeted a bit. "Why don't we have some more wine while I make dinner, then we can talk more afterward," he said finally.

Rami put a hand on Henri's shoulder. They seemed to silently communicate something to each other. "Yes, let us talk more after dinner."

"What can I do to help?" I asked.

Henri said, "You can work on the rice. Take out an onion from there, dice it up. Spices are there: cumin, paprika, cayenne, salt, pepper. I will be right back. I need to get the wood going."

He was gone for ten minutes. I took out the spices and started on the onion. Rami looked on, enjoying his wine. Clearly, he was not going to help.

When Henri came back inside, he smelled of smoke. "Hickory?" I wondered.

"All right, the wood is going. I need raisins and almonds to toast," he said, looking over what I had done.

"That is good with the onion. In the big pot there, with butter, and sauté them until they just start to see through." He turned the heat up on the pot while I got the butter and onions in. Then he took a smaller pan and quickly toasted the almonds and set those aside. He toasted the rice next.

Once the onions were ready, the rice and spices were next. Then bone broth pulled from the fridge was poured in. "Let that simmer but not boil. I will be right back with the wood." he instructed.

I checked on the rice, watching it until he came back. Shortly he returned with a bucket full of smoldering wood and glowing charcoal.

"Lift the grill side up, please?" he asked and when I did, he poured the smoking mass onto the grill side of the stovetop. The woodsmoke smelled wonderful.

After that, he cooked the goat kebabs over the coals, until the corners had a nice char. It smelled wonderful, everything smelled so wonderful. Once the rice was done, in went the almonds and raisins, then it was all poured out into a heap on a platter.

"Mmm...so fragrant," I said.

I was getting really hungry as he pushed the meat off the skewers and on top of the rice. Out came some steaming flatbread from the oven. I didn't even see him put those in.

Rami looked giddy with excitement as Henri carried the platter over to the table. "Just plates from there, if you please. No silverware is used unless you really feel you need it."

"Okay." I did not. I was fine without it.

We all sat down and refilled our wine. "Salut," Henri said, and we raised our glasses.

"Oh my god, Henri, this smells so good," I said.

We both looked at Rami as he tore off a piece of bread and used it to pick up a chunk of meat and scoop some rice. Into his mouth it went. There was a lot of that, followed by lip smacking as we all tucked in. The meat was so tender and that smoky char with that fragrant dry spice rub. It was the best goat I had ever had, too. The meal consisted of mostly chewing and groaning.

"Better than my mother's—there is no shame in saying this. Mother, please forgive me," Rami said, looking up at the ceiling.

Henri grinned as I said, "This is the best goat I have ever had. This wine with it, the food, everything tastes and smells so wonderful. What a meal."

"A toast to the chef, to this wonderful meal, and to meeting you, Lauren," Rami said as we all raised our glasses again.

After we had filled our bellies, Rami stepped out for a cigarette while Henri and I cleared the table.

"Thank you, Henri," I said, "for helping me and making me feel welcome." I kissed him on the cheek. I was feeling warm from the wine, and he smelled so good. For a moment I wanted to do it again on the mouth and much harder. I wanted to *taste* his mouth.

I felt all flushed, my nipples turning rock-hard in an instant when one rubbed against his forearm. It was electric. I felt a rapidly growing tension in my belly.

He sensed this change and stepped away from me, to put the pot up on the rack. He stepped back further again and began drying his hands with a towel. "This is going to be hard, I think. But it is not right, we do not even know each other."

I was so embarrassed. "No, no, I'm sorry," I said. "I'm... This is so new, and these feelings and sensations are so powerful. I am just feeling overwhelmed."

"Perhaps a walk then in the cool night air?" he offered.

"Yeah, that might be best," I agreed as I exhaled loudly, maybe a little too loudly. Rami was just coming in.

"How about a walk, Rami?" I asked.

He inhaled deeply and then looked at us, his eyes narrowing a bit as he chuckled under his breath and said, "Oh yes of course, it's a very good idea."

I crossed my arms, hiding my throbbing nipples, and nodded.

Chapter Three

The night was clear and breezy, and there was only a sliver of a moon. But we could all see clearly and quite far as our eyes adjusted to the dark. "It is just a mile into town," Henri said. Napoleon followed along after us.

"Okay, why don't you tell me how you came to be Made then," I said, looking at him.

We walked a little farther and he began to speak. "The town I lived in was mostly fishermen and farmers. It was very quiet and peaceful. There were ruins in the water from Roman times along the shore where we played. I was the third and youngest boy in my family. We farmed and fished, and caught spider crabs that I loved to eat. They were my favorite.

"When I was twelve, word came that there was a cathedral being built in Le Havre and the opportunity to be apprenticed as a mason was a rare chance for anyone. I had only been to a city twice. It was huge, people everywhere. It was also dirty and smelled unbelievably bad most of the time. The work itself was horribly hard. Heavy backbreaking labor was what I was initially relegated to. The old church was built one hundred years before we started work. The ground it was built on was not good. Very unstable, all the workmen knew this but the monk who was overseeing the project would not hear it. He was determined to see his grand design made real. But the walls he wanted built were just too high.

"He worked us nearly to death, haunting the structure at night to inspect and criticize the workmanship. There were many accidents, and I was hurt many, many times.

"One night a great storm blew in from the sea. The wind was the worst I had ever seen, and the rain was coming down so hard. It tore the leaves from the trees. All the streets were flooded. Soon the ground was saturated, and the walls began to sway. This monk, his name was Jabati, began screaming for additional support beams to be placed. He whipped us when we were not moving fast enough, shouting obscenities that no man of God should ever utter." He shook his head.

"He shoved me out of the way as I struggled with a beam too big for me to move myself and tried pushing it into place on his own. I tripped and fell flat on my face, breaking my nose for the first time." He touched his nose gingerly.

"As I rolled over our legs got tangled. He tripped and fell on top of me. I tried to push him off and get up, but a great boom shook the wall and it collapsed over us. I was small and fit between a large stone block and the beam that had fallen across. But my arms were pinned with Jabati on top. He was crushed by the stones." He looked down, shaking his head again.

"I was trapped there until the workers were able to clear the debris the next day. They could not believe that I had survived. My right arm was broken, and my left was badly mangled. I was in a very bad way. The nuns took care of me and cleaned my wounds. They set the bone. They prayed over me for days, certain that my arms would have to be cut off if gangrene set in. Miraculously I began to recover. I could no longer work so I was sent home to heal. I returned to farmwork for a while before going back to Le Havre." He paused and looked up at the stars for a moment.

"I did not transition until I was in my twenties. By then I had returned to work in the same cathedral and was finishing my apprenticeship. The new priest overseeing the project made many changes from the previous design. Much lower walls that the unstable ground would hold. I was introduced to baroque design after that."

He closed his eyes for a moment and said, "I started having headaches and sensitivity to light. We slaughtered animals daily to cook and eat. The smell of the fresh blood grew more and more enticing. The aroma made my mouth water, and my stomach would ache and growl. I thought I was going crazy. One day I slaughtered a goat for the evening meal, and I just couldn't help myself. I started licking the blood off my fingers and the blade I used to cut the goat's throat with. It made the headaches go away for a little while. I started sipping it in small quantities after that. The more I drank the better I felt. It took a while for me to figure out how much I needed. I had to hide this from everyone. I knew if anyone found out I was drinking blood I would be branded a witch. But I did in the end find a good way to hide this. I began to have a growing appreciation for the subtle nuance of flavors in many of the spices the work camp cooks used. In my free time I started to ask questions and help in the kitchens. Everyone just thought I was looking for a wife. What I really wanted to do was learn how to make blood sausage. This was a staple food back then. Once I learned how to prepare it, I felt safe. No one questioned it when I would collect blood to make a fresh batch or tasted it uncooked to check if the spices were right. I used the same blend of spices in the flask of blood you drank Lauren." He looked at me and smiled then continued his story.

"Most of the great cathedrals being built ran operations throughout the day and night. I transitioned to a life of mostly night work. I moved around a lot then, following the work.

"Before I knew it, thirty years had passed. I still looked like I was in my early twenties when I was forty. That was old back then. My father died when he was forty-two and my mother when she was thirty-eight. Life was very hard," he said.

"By then I was a master mason and carpenter. And a very good cook. I had an interest in metalworking and began training as a blacksmith. I burned my hands and arms so many times. I always healed well, though." He flexed his muscular arms.

"I moved to New Canada. Modern-day Quebec in 1744. Ten years before the French and Indian War that eventually became the Seven Years' War. I fought in this war against the British. But in the end, they took New Canada, and I lost my wife and infant son."

"I met Rami then. He was the only other one of us I had ever met. He helped me work through the grief and loss." He was looking down as he said this.

Rami chimed in at this point. "Yes, I met Henri then. I was sent to the Americas to begin documenting stories and rumors of others like us. Ah, we have arrived."

We walked the distance to the town center of Gilead. Only a few streetlights were on. One was near a small red building that we were walking toward.

Henri began to speak again as he pointed at the building. "I helped build this station when the railroad was built in 1851. It wasn't built here, though, it was moved here later. I had been working the log river runs in the 1820s and '30s. Driving logs down the river to the coast. It was hard work."

We walked up to the building, and as we looked in the window he pointed at the far wall. There was a historical display inside. Some tools, railroad spikes and a section of rail. There was also some maps and a few faded pictures of the workmen.

"That one has me in it, third man from the left." The photo was of a group of men standing onshore in front of a large raft of logs that were used to make the railroad ties. I looked and that was definitely him. He didn't seem to have changed much other than his hair was longer.

"I'd traveled through here again in 1841 and decided it was where I really wanted to be," he said, pointing across the way to a stand of light-colored trees. I thought they might be birches. "Over there is a grove of trees that the town is named after, balm of Gilead. It is a type of poplar. The wood is not good for much, but the buds exude a sticky resin that has medicinal properties. The native peoples used it in their medicines. That is not what they called it, either. I have always loved their scent in the summer air."

"It's so strange to me," I said. "The concept of living so long, to see the world change around you." I shook my head.

Rami said, "It takes getting used to. It took a good hundred years before I came to grips with those feelings. It can sometimes be a very lonely and sad existence. Seeing people we love and care for grow old and pass. But at the same time, we perceive the world differently, having a much broader view."

We walked a loop through town and headed back.

***

Rami began his story, taking a long drag off his cigarette. "I was born in Málaga, Spain, in 1482. The valley was so wonderful. My family had orchards. It was such a beautiful place." His eyes sparkled in the moonlight. I could see there was love and loss there.

"The Christian nobles of Europe had been at war with us for centuries. My people crossed over from North Africa and took the Iberian Peninsula almost seven hundred years before in a very bloody war. We brought science, philosophy, architecture, and Islam with us. The Christians banded together and had been pushing back for hundreds of years." He paused and lit another cigarette.

After a long draw and exhalation of smoke, he continued. "My father was killed in a skirmish when I was six and my mother and I fled to Granada when fighting grew too close to our home. Granada, our last great stronghold. I was always a very smart boy. I could read by the time I was four, count remarkably high and do simple math. In Granada there was a sanctuary where a great scholar lived. Every five years a boy would be selected to be his retainer. I was chosen for this. It was very strange at first. A tower within a walled compound within another walled compound." He dropped his cigarette and stepped on it.

"Everyone called him Ibn Al'Masoud, the Gift of Allah. Everyone knew he was centuries old and attributed his longevity to be a blessing from Allah." He shook his head.

"They did not know the truth. He was more than centuries old; he was almost two thousand years old. He was very frail, but his mind! I have never met such a towering intellect in all my time." He raised a finger in the air.

"He was a contemporary of Aristotle. Some called him the Oracle. The caliph protected him from the world. His insights and wisdom were highly treasured. I would take him to a special room in the keep with a series of thick steel grates mounted in a wall. The caliph, his advisers, judges, and many other important and powerful people would come and ask him questions or advice. You see, he could speak and read dozens of languages, many of them dead. He would decipher ancient tomes and scrolls and translate them. Scribes would sit on the other side of the grate and write everything down. When he spoke, you could feel the weight of the centuries in every word." He shook his head again and took a deep breath before continuing.

"I was the only person allowed to have physical contact with him. I slept in a small bed in his chambers. Each day I would bring a goat or lamb in. I would help him slaughter the animal in accordance with halal practices. He would drain the blood and drink it before preparing the meat. He told me it was what kept him alive for so long. His diet was simple: fruits and vegetables, lamb or goat, bread and cheese. All of these I would bring in each day. I helped him dress and wash his clothes. I attended to all his needs.

"He read a great deal, and his library was extraordinary. There were hundreds of books and scrolls all neatly organized. His agreement with the caliph was that he was allowed to keep all the originals that they sent him to translate. There were many original books written by all the great and forgotten philosophers. From him I learned to read and write in Greek, Latin, Hebrew, and Aramaic. He was very kind and patient and treated me very, very well. While he could not replace my father, he came very close. Such was my love and admiration for him. In 1491 it was clear that the combined Christian nations would eventually win, so the rest of the Muslim nations abandoned us.

"In December of that year there were many battles and skirmishes. I heard very little of this in the depths of the keep." He looked up at the heavens for a moment before continuing.

"I was preparing him a lunch of figs, cheese, and bread. He loved figs. He was in his library. I was bringing his tray to him when out of nowhere an errant cannonball struck the tower, shattering the iron grates in the window and exploding into the room. I was knocked unconscious."

"I was so disoriented when I came to. There was pain, and so much smoke. And the books, the treasured books and scrolls and maps he'd collected for nearly two thousand years were aflame. The knowledge of the ages from the greatest minds of the previous millennium were burning. My head hurt, and my hand was gashed open.

"I crawled to his chair. It was very smoky. He lay on his back, his face bleeding and with a piece of twisted metal impaling him through the sternum. He was feeling around himself, unable to move his legs. I reached out and took his hand, and he clutched it.

"He pulled me to him and looked at my wounded hand. Then whispered, 'My legacy is now you. My legacy is now you.' Turning his head to look at me, he gripped the metal with his other hand and wrenched it free. There was so much blood. Then he held my wounded hand to the ragged hole in his chest, all the while whispering, 'My legacy...my legacy is in the blood.' I tried to pull away, but he held me fast.

"He grew weaker and weaker until he passed."

"I wrapped my hand up and gathered a few of the books into a basket, dragging it through the keep until I made it to the portal where they passed the goats to me. It was locked. I banged and banged on it, but no one could hear. It seemed like days before someone came and finally unlocked it. Then there was a commotion as men on the other side were shouting for the Oracle. I unlocked my side, and they pulled me through. I told him that the Oracle was dead. I was covered in his blood and soot; I must have been a sight. The men carried me away, leaving the books behind in the basket. I was never able to go back and save them." He shook his head again you could see the pain and loss in his eyes.

"Then, on the second of January of 1492, the caliph surrendered Granada to the Christian forces. I was returned to my mother later that month. Many fled Spain but most of us stayed. We were forced to renounce Allah and convert to the Christian faith or die. It was a terrible time."

He raised his finger and smiled. "But we got to keep our orchards, at least at first. When I was a teenager, the Spanish Inquisition began. It was meant to catch and find those of us that had converted to Christianity who were still following Islam in secret. They came for us and the Jews as well. They tortured and killed the educated and the learned. Calling them heretics and witches in an attempt to quash knowledge of the past and eliminate our traditions from the public consciousness. It is easier to control the uneducated masses, keep them in fear, work them to the bone, while the coffers of the royals and church grow fat off their labors. It is a pattern repeated so many times, across the ages even today."

I put my hand on his shoulder. "That is awful. I am so sorry," I said.

He nodded and patted my hand and then continued. "Men came looking for me when I was sixteen; the Circle had sent them. It took a long time for them to track me down. I had not transitioned yet and had fled to Tunisia. They took me across Europe to the Balkans.

"There was a castle high in the mountains that was controlled by the Circle. The Oracle had been a member of the Circle. I found out that the Circle was many thousands of years old. They treated me well and wanted me to retell everything that had occurred from the day I was first sent to the Oracle. They too lamented the loss of the library. Once they knew I had been anointed in the Oracle's blood, they wanted me to stay to see if I would eventually transition. I stayed with them, and I learned so much about their operations and means of communication, their mission and history. They appreciated my quick mind and valued the lineage I now bore when I finally transitioned. The Oracle had been the oldest among them. There were many who were Made that served them in what was called the Ring."

"This was before the Prohibition that outlawed the practice. Many had been Made in the past or were Born without guidance that fed off other humans instead of animals. Most were driven to madness by the killings and slaughter. They are the origin of the vampire myths."

"I was eventually made one of their emissaries. We would search for and hunt those of our kind who had taken this dark path. I found that I was very good at hunting and tracking them down."

"We were cultivating contacts across the globe. Ultimately, I was sent to the Americas. We had no contact with any of the indigenous population on either of the American continents at that time. I was looking forward to meeting them, learning more about their culture and histories. I had met Henri in Quebec. We traveled together for a while but at last I needed to continue my mission. We have remained close friends and keep in regular contact." Here he paused briefly before continuing.

"During World War II, the Nazis began to experiment on people, Jews and any of the other peoples they deemed inferior. The Circle saw what might happen should they discover any of us and somehow create an army of immortals. We heal so quickly, and our heightened senses make us exceptionally good natural hunters. The Circle prohibited Making and did their best to help move both Born and Made out of Europe. We had infiltrated most of the higher levels of the European governments and their newly created intelligence services, including Nazi Germany. Using this intelligence, we were successful in preventing them from creating a master race. It truly could have been a disastrous and monstrous outcome." He finished speaking as we had walked all the way back to the house.

***

"Well, I suppose it is my turn then," I said. "Shall we sit out here?"

"Yes, that would be nice," Rami agreed.

Henri nodded and asked, "Anyone thirsty?"

"Oh yes, please. One of your Bloody Marys would be lovely," said Rami.

"Me too," I responded as Rami took out a small silver cigarette case.

"Do you mind if I smoke while we sit?" he asked.

"No, that is fine. Everyone smoked in Afghanistan. But I was not there long," I said as I settled into a lounge chair.

Henri returned shortly with a tray and three of the house specialties. "That smells so good," I told him. We spent the next few minutes sipping the bloody concoctions.

"All right then, I guess it is my turn." I started and suddenly stopped. "Wait, you don't even know my last name, do you?" They both shook their heads. "Well, that is awkward. Lauren Elizabeth Cortez. Nice to meet you both?" We toasted.

"I am twenty-two, twenty-three next week on my birthday. I am originally from—well, I was born in Virginia. My mother is from here, up in Fort Fairfield, Aroostook County. My dad was from California. He was in the army so 'we' were in the army. We moved around a lot. I've lived in Germany, Texas, Georgia,

Washington, Virginia. I've traveled across Europe, and I have been to Afghanistan.

"My dad was just a year out from retirement when he was killed by a drunk driver while walking across the street. Multiple in-theater deployments and a drunk kid is what killed him." I sighed and shook my head.

"We had been looking to buy a home for his retirement at the time. I had just one year left in high school. Our lives really went sideways after that. The insurance paid out and Mom used it to drink herself to death. So that was a mess." I sighed heavily again.

"I'm so sorry to hear this, Lauren," Rami said as Henri nodded.

"I had always been athletic. I was a runner, I tried gymnastics, but I was a bit too tall, and I started too late. I never really liked team sports anyway. I preferred to compete against my best time or distance.

"Anyway, my grades took a hit with what was going on with my mom after Dad died. I barely graduated and didn't know what to do. I was alone. I did not feel ready for college or know what I even wanted to study. I started community college anyway off my dad's GI Bill. But after a year I knew it wasn't for me. I just felt lost, so I took a break and traveled around a bit visiting relatives."

"I ended up visiting my grandfather in California. He was retired from the army and hailed from a long line of servicemen. I really liked him. We spent a month talking and traveling around California. I finally decided to join the army and serve my country. I did well. I really enjoyed the training and that feeling of a shared mission and comradery. Basic training was fun, and I was starting to feel really fulfilled and satisfied with my choice." I took a long sip from my drink before continuing.

"I was scheduled to deploy to Afghanistan. A couple of weeks before I left, we had been training hard and I really started to feel run-down. It sort of came and went and came and went. Each time it was a little worse. I began getting headaches. I toughed it out, though. I didn't want to be left behind.

"I was sent to Baghran and then an FOB from there. I had literally been there for a week. The headaches were worse with the altitude. We were escorting friendlies back to their village. The terrain was mountainous, with narrow trails and thin tree cover mostly. We got them to their village easy-peasy. The drones swept the valley for the trip back and we were in the clear. Intel was good. We were about two klicks out from the FOB. Alpha team was about a klick ahead. We brought up the rear in the Bravo unit. Six-man teams, the sarge and RO in the middle. Larry and Moe were on point. I was on the left flank and Davis was on the right. We came to a village we had previously passed through. The villagers were there when we'd come around the first time—a boy with goats, a woman and her two daughters—but not when we went back. I had turned to check out our six and noticed the sun going down. I was only distracted for a few seconds but when I turned back—*wham!*—I was hit from above. Turns out it was a guy. He broke both my collarbones, stabbed me in the upper back on the way down. Missed my spine by an inch but it punctured a lung. I was lucky my gear protected me...well, mostly. He slashed my face for good measure too. There was automatic gunfire. I assume Davis the machine gunner had opened fire. I blacked out from the pain." I shook my head.

"When I woke up shortly after I was in a cave. The walls were stone. There were bodies everywhere. The boy, the woman, her daughters. My guys and two of the guys who attacked us; there were two of them still upright." I choked up a bit. I hated reliving this, but I dream about it every night.

"I just need a second," I said. "I have PTSD and talking about this makes me anxious." They both looked concerned for me, nodding that they understood.

After a few minutes I continued. "It was a nightmarish scene. There was blood everywhere. The two men were dressed like the locals. They were tearing the clothes off one of the kids and licking the blood from the wounds. They had gloves on with razors sewn in along the fingers. It's what my face was slashed with." I touched the scar on my chin.

"I think they thought I must be dead or were saving me for last. I don't know why they didn't kill me like the others. I was hurt badly but I managed to get my sidearm out and up. When they turned to look at me, I could not believe it—their eyes glowed in the lantern light like a coyote's. They screeched at me and their teeth were sharp like an animal's. I got one in the chest and the other through the neck before blowing his jaw off. They both landed on top of me and we struggled as they bled out.

"I was trapped under them and passed out at some point. The Alpha team found us a little while later. They discovered a tunnel under the hut in the village where the little girls lived; the men had dragged everyone down there. I woke up on the medevac. Shipped out to Germany, then…finally home."

"Their teeth? Sharp and pointy like a dog's or triangular like a shark's?" Rami asked, looking suddenly genuinely concerned.

"Uh…triangles, like they filed them into points maybe?" I said.

"Yes, that is what I was getting at. And how many did you count of these men?"

"I'm not sure. There were at least two on the ground near me and the two I killed."

"Kazim...this is very bad." Rami shook his head. "If the cult of Kazim is active again, this is very, very bad."

Both Henri and I asked at the same time: "Who is Kazim?"

***

Rami gave a long sigh and then explained. "During the Crusades, which occurred between the years 1100 and the beginning of the 1200s, a sect of fanatical Islamic warriors rose to prominence in Persia and in Syria. They were called the Hashashin; it is the origin of the word "assassin." They used drug-filled rituals to prepare for their murder missions. Utterly ruthless and fearless men, totally devoted to their leader, Nizari Ismai'ili. I do not recall the exact date, but the Mongol army was spreading across Asia led by Genghis Khan. They clashed with the Hashashin and took control of the castle they were based out of, destroying the cult and killing Nizari. It is unknown how many survived but at least one did who was thought to be one of his most fervent devotees. His name was only ever known as Kazim. It is believed that he is a Born, but it might be possible that he was Made. He fled to another mountain stronghold in Afghanistan and used what he learned from Nizari to create a small army of devoted cutthroats for hire.

"He starved his recruits, warped their minds with drugs. Made them fight each other until only the strongest four survived. Then he rewarded each of them with his blood, making them into one of us. It is said he cut several of his own ribs out, ground them up, and pressed them into a wound he gave to each of his chosen ones. Each of his devotees would then do the same and so on.

"The rumors of the size of his army vary but given the number and types of attacks he is attributed to, the estimate is around two hundred. One of their trademarks was filing their teeth into points, like a shark's tooth. We have a skull of one in Geneva. They wore no armor but were known for sewing knives, needles, and spikes into their clothing. Elbows, knees, every surface had a blade, or some means of causing harm. Often, they used poisons that they would take small doses of regularly to build up a tolerance and coated the blades with the same. It was extremely dangerous to engage them with any handheld weapons. They did not block, parry, or feint, instead rushing in quickly to close with their opponents. Even when wounded they would slash with their arms, hands, and feet, kicking and biting. They seemed immune to pain. Or at least that's how the story goes.

"It is said they screeched like the banshee to strike fear in those they were approaching. The Circle made many attempts to contact Kazim as well as to infiltrate his group. He or his men killed every single one of our representatives. Kazim worked only for the many warlords who controlled the drug trade across Asia. We know he operated in and around what is now Afghanistan and Pakistan. His activities ceased in the mid-1800s, and nothing more was ever heard of him again. It is very concerning to think that he or one of his followers has reestablished the Cult. But where you were attacked is the right area of the world. We have a huge database of genetic material we've collected over time to trace any of us who has ever existed. I would implore you to let us have a sample of your marrow to see if the Makers DNA you carry is from Kazim's lineage." Rami folded his hands and waited for a response.

"I...if it will help, then yes," I said with a shrug.

"Excellent. I have everything I need in the car. I have done this many, many times," he said.

"What! Right now? I mean, okay. Will it...will it hurt much?"

"Yes, it will sting actually, but not for long."

"That doesn't really make me feel any better." I'm not sure whether I should laugh, cry, or just run.

"I will give you something for the pain. But it will only hurt for a day or so," he said.

"Are you a doctor too?" I asked.

"No, but I did sleep in a Holiday Inn Express last week so you should be fine." He said this with a straight face, his eyes twinkling with glee. Then he laughed aloud. He was definitely not making me feel any better.

"I'm so sorry. I have always wanted to say that," he apologized. Then he got up and went to his car but quickly returned. "We should go inside. It is not very sterile out here."

"Well, I wasn't going to let you do it out here." I was a bit flushed, not sure what exactly I had just agreed to. Henri didn't say much but he didn't seem nervous.

"All right then. There are several locations from which I can draw what I need, either sternum or hip. I will clean the skin and numb the site, then use a wide bore needle to punch through the bone. I only need one cc, so it will be very quick."

"Well, sternum then," I said.

He took out a prep kit: a large needle and syringe, and one of those vacutainer tubes that they draw labs into. He handed me a bubble cap pill.

"This is a broad-spectrum antibiotic; you should take it now. I have some lidocaine to numb the skin, but it will not help with the bone," he explained.

"I think I'll skip that," I said, taking the pill with a sip of Bloody Mary.

"As you wish. If you open your shirt then and remove your bra, I will prepare the site." Both men looked away as I unbuttoned my shirt. The bra was a front loader so that helped.

I cupped "the girls," one in each hand. "Okay, I'm ready."

The prep was cold, and he scrubbed the spot well. "All right. You will feel a pinch, some pressure, and then a dull ache. I will be quick. I am sorry about this. I should not have made light of it earlier. Your scent makes me feel...awkward. Like a schoolboy. A man my age should know better. I am embarrassed."

"It's okay. Let's just get it over with."

With a gloved hand, he felt around for some landmark that I could not see, then pushed the needle in. It only stung a bit. He had to twist it a little as he put pressure on it to penetrate the bone. *That* stung like a wasp sting and made me gasp.

He drew back on the plunger and when he had enough pulled the needle out. He had a gauze pad ready.

"Henri, will you put pressure here, please?" He held the needle while he aspirated the contents into the tube, shook it up, and slipped it into a plastic container.

"There we are. Let me have a look." He took the gauze away and there was some bloody ooze.

"Keep pressure on it for another few minutes, then a Band-Aid will suffice. Thank you, Lauren. You do not know how valuable your donation will be to the Circle and to our shared cause," he said.

"It's okay. It wasn't that bad really."

"Are you sure you're okay?" Henri asked and I nodded in the affirmative.

"All right then. I guess I will call it a night," I said. "I have a lot to think about." Cupping my boobs still. "If you boys don't mind, I think I'll head upstairs and get some sleep."

"Do you need anything?" Henri asked.

"God, he smells good," I thought. I could think of a couple of things I'd have him do to help me get to sleep. But he was right, we really didn't know each other. I know I blushed again when he asked.

I just shook my head no. It felt weird standing there holding my boobs in my hands in front of them both.

As I started up the stairs I called back. "Good night." They echoed the same in reply. I could hear them talking as Rami put his things away and I buttoned up my shirt.

Napoleon followed me all the way to my room. I asked him if he wanted to come in. He padded across the room and sat on the bed.

"Okay, then. You are not shy, are you?" His tail thumped on the bed. I got ready for sleep and slid in between the sheets next to him.

"Ahhhh." That was the one thing I missed the most when I was in the army: a big comfortable bed, and nice cool sheets. It didn't take me long to fall asleep and for the first time in a very long time, I did not dream of the attack. I do not even remember what I dreamed.

***

Napoleon was right there where I left him in the morning.

"Well, hello, handsome," I said. He lifted his head and panted as his tail thumped against the bed. I felt my sternum. It ached but only just a little. Napoleon walked over to the door and looked back at me expectantly. "Does someone have to pee?" I let him out, got dressed, and went downstairs.

I appeared to be the only one up. Napoleon nudged the front door open while I rummaged around in the kitchen. Henri had a very complex-looking espresso machine that I didn't have the wherewithal to try to use without first studying the field manual. I did find some OJ in the fridge. There was a bag of croissants in the pantry, as well as some jam and butter, and I was all set.

After breakfast I walked out front to check on the dog and noticed Rami's car was gone. I caught a whiff of Henri in the breeze and turned my nose in that direction. He was walking back toward the house from the fields pushing a large wheelbarrow. He raised a hand in good morning and headed toward the barn with the animal stalls. I raised my hand in greeting and followed along. "Do you need help?"

"Sure," he said. "I've put out feed and just need to clean the stalls and put down new hay. The animals stay out in the fields most of the time. But it is going to rain most of the week. So I wanted to make their stalls ready if they wanted to come back inside." We spent the next hour working in the barn. It was fun. We laughed…a lot.

Later on I asked where Rami had gone.

"He left last night because he wanted to get the sample to the lab. There's a note for you on the table with his contact information."

"Okay," I said. "I hope my contribution helps in some way."

We spent the next few days just working on his farm. He showed me around the area. We took drives through the mountains of western Maine, got ice cream. It was calm and peaceful. I felt the tight knot of tension in my gut slowly begin to unravel. My life the last few years had been a whirlwind of loss, regret, pain, and fear. While I frequently had the urge to tear off Henri's clothes, I was getting used to his smell a little bit at a time. I had fallen in love with Napoleon. He had slept with me every night and was right there every morning so happy to see me wake up.

I called the few friends I had who'd messaged me as I had been offline a while, telling them I had been shacking up with this cool French guy on his farm and was thinking of becoming a hippie. It seemed easier than saying I was a vampire now and spent my days drinking slightly alcoholic real blood Bloody Marys and tending sheep.

One morning we were having breakfast. Henri had cooked some bacon from a pig he slaughtered and eggs from the girls out front, and also crusty baguettes he'd made himself, when a thought occurred to me.

"Do you think that Kazim's men didn't cut me up like the others because I smelled like one of them?" I asked. Henri stopped mid-bite and thought about it.

He chewed quickly and swallowed. "That seems plausible, if they had never been exposed to any others, Born or Made; it may have confused them. Especially a female. The way you smelled may have been a factor. Or they were just saving you for dessert since you smelled so good." He laughed with a cute little *tut tut* chortling sound.

I changed the subject. "Do I smell good? Rami seemed to think so."

"Yes, yes you do, you smell very good to me. It is distracting sometimes, but it is very pleasant having you here and having you near me. I was getting a bit lonely recently. That was why I went down to Portland to take a few odd jobs. Meet some people, feel connected to the world again even if only for a little while. Our kind tend to be loners, inclined to lead lonely lives. You must find things you enjoy, things to fill the endless days and nights."

"Have you thought of leaving and just traveling again?" I asked.

"I had actually thought about it. I have been here a long time; I have these moments. We all do, but they pass."

"Well, I am glad you found me and that I came here. I feel so much better. I felt caught in some horrible spiral, getting sicker and feeling worse every day. I felt like…I felt like a car that was idling way too fast. You know, when you're in an old car doing that. You just tap the gas pedal, and it returns to a normal idle speed? That's how it feels. I was just idling too fast and now I just…don't," I said, smiling.

"I am glad you shared that with me. I am glad to know you are feeling better." He reached over and squeezed my hand.

We cleaned up the dishes. There was a lot to do keeping up his farm. He was glad for the help and gave me time to think about what to do next.

A week later Rami called with some news. "Hello, Lauren, do you have a moment to speak to me?"

I was just sitting and reading on the front porch. "Yes, of course."

"Very good, then. Do you feel up to air travel?" he asked.

"Uh, yes, I suppose so. What is this about?"

"The Circle would very much like to make your acquaintance," he answered. "In Geneva this coming weekend. You would be flown there on a private jet."

"Oh...uh. I don't have a current passport. I haven't renewed it since I got out," I said.

"I have arranged for one to be issued for you. It will arrive by courier tomorrow," he said.

"Oh. Um...can I think about it? I mean, is it something that's required of me to be part of the Ring?"

"Oh yes, my dear, you may refuse. You are not obliged to do anything you do not want to do or are uncomfortable with. I understand that you are going through quite a few changes and things may seem overwhelming. Please think it over and give me a call back. I can make travel arrangements within twenty-four hours."

"Okay, I will think it over and give you a call back in the next few days," I said.

"Good, very good. Have a lovely day, Lauren. Say hello to Henri for me, please."

"I will, thanks," I said and hung up.

Henri was out in the garage gassing up the dirt bikes. We were going to load them up for a ride along the river. "Hey, Henri. Rami called. He says hello," I told him.

"Oh, I was wondering when we were going to hear from him. Any news on that sample that you volunteered?"

"No, he didn't mention that. But the Circle? They want me to fly to Geneva to meet them. Does that sound weird to you?" I asked.

He pondered that for a minute. "No, that sounds about right. My understanding is that they always want to meet with any newly Born."

"Oh." I frowned. "Okay. It's just...it felt weird. Rami already got me a new passport. It will be here tomorrow."

Chapter Four

Geneva, Switzerland

"What do you think, could she be the One, Ellis?" Martin, the lanky, dapper-looking redhead, asked. His accent was faintly British.

"It is definitely possible. Her lineage comes from the right region of France where we know the nurse Claudette Paschette lived and operated for at least a hundred years. It is the right time frame. There are many, many other variables to consider," Ellis said, closing the report binder.

He tucked the binder under his arm, then stood and walked to the window. He loved the view of Geneva at night.

"It will not be long before we have a detailed gene map and can verify what we hope we will find. If she is not the One, then she is the closest we may ever come." He turned to look at Martin.

The two were obviously brothers, with the same tall lanky frame and bone structure. They shared the same father but different mothers. One Italian, the other Welsh. Both had short curly hair, Martin's red and Ellis's jet-black. They both appeared to be in their late twenties but were much older than that, having been Made during the first World War.

"We make no moves until we know for sure. There is a great deal at risk if we are wrong," Ellis said, walking over to the open wall safe. He placed the preliminary report marked "Curvel" in the stack of other folders there and removed a silk-wrapped object. He pulled back the covering to reveal an ancient-looking woodcut; the face of the woman was nearly identical to Lauren's. He rewrapped it and placed it back in the safe, closing the door and spinning the lock, then resetting the alarm.

"I have a team standing by. Hopefully she will voluntarily help; if not we will take what we need." Ellis walked across the room and finished his wine.

Martin stood and nodded. "Very good, then. The final report from Su'wasee is in. The Afghanistan venture was not a complete failure and all the recruits have been accounted for and eliminated. Their bodies prepared for the attack. Hopefully very soon we can begin phase three. I will have Su'wasee eliminated once the funds are transferred, and we have taken delivery. There will be no connection to our operation." Ellis smiled and nodded.

He had waited a long time for this opportunity. If he could not find "Eve," one of her daughters would have to suffice.

"Let me know the moment you hear something," he said, leaving Martin to his work.

His security team was waiting outside the door, grim-looking men in bulky suits. He felt like a gazelle walking among rhinos.

Martin checked the software program he'd written, a limited AI. He had backdoored the security systems of all the major and a few minor social media platforms. Those he could not break into he had paid a pretty penny for someone else to do it.

The facial recognition software was scanning continuously looking for her. Hundreds of millions of photos and video feeds were being sifted through. Hundreds of possible hits popped up daily, each one carefully researched to see if they were viable hits. The rise in genealogy websites with their vast, ever-expanding databases were a trove of information. He had already found forty-three new promising familial bloodlines that crisscrossed every continent. All distant relatives of his Maker and the other Born.

He found Lauren's lineage very interesting. Preliminary results showed that it was an intersection of four Curvel bloodlines. There was a high probability that she would be a potent Maker. Her progeny could live longer than most. At least that was his hope. More time. The wish of every man, woman, and child that had ever lived. Just a little more time.

The Made were no different. Why be satisfied with a tenfold extension when a twenty-fold extension of their lives might be possible? Or even more if their theory on Eve was in fact true. His computer models tracing bloodlines showed that a single woman, their "Eve," estimated at more than 20,000 years old, could still be living today. That she has had children repeatedly in different locations and times across history. The most recent one was two hundred years ago in France. If she was alive, he would do anything to find her. He had a plan, the means to support it, and the time it might take to see it through. Once every detail of the plan was checked over twice, he turned to the window and looked up at the night sky.

Southern Afghanistan

Su'wasee stood at the entrance to the caves. Three long refrigerated trucks under heavy guard passed her by. Once they were clear she removed her hijab and discarded it. Her alliance with Ellis and Martin had paid off big. She checked her account balances. This morning it was $13,450,000. The new balance was $33,450,000. She smiled, something she rarely did, and shut the phone off, then walked back inside.

Her men did not look up; they were already dismantling the liquid nitrogen tanks and tubs they used to flash-freeze the bodies with. The men were hauling the equipment to a deep pit in the cave and dumping it in.

The walls of this cavern were dotted with walkways and tunnels leading in every direction. It had been her grandfather Kazim's base of operation. Kazim's men had dug and scratched out hundreds of rooms and chambers over the many centuries.

The ceiling was black and caked with soot from centuries of torches that burned in the sconces along the hall. She climbed the long winding steps to the Pleasure Palace. Kazim had created a harem where hundreds of women and girls, mostly kidnapped or bought, were kept for his most faithful servants to use, and abuse.

She paused just inside and closed her eyes. The cries, screams, and moans seemed to echo from the many alcoves and hallways. The women once used up were discarded like trash into the same pit the equipment was being dumped in. She imagined the thousands of bodies rotting there, all the men who were killed by their brothers as they fought for the great prize: immortality. Nothing really changed when her father killed her grandfather

Kazim and took control of the operation. He stole immortality rather than earn it.

He only shifted the focus away from hired killers to moving the drug lords' goods, storing them safely until they sold and releasing them to the buyer. It was a good model, but eventually the American military began encroaching on them, disrupting supply lines. The need to hold the drugs in secure locations was abandoned. Still, her father managed to hang on to a small army of devotees and scaled back the operations.

Su had been lucky, as she was sent away to school in the UK, where she had an interest in medicine, in studying the thing in the blood that kept the men—including her grandfather and father—alive so long. Having started off in medicine she then moved on to genetics. She had no desire to take care of people or make them well again; her interests were purely selfish. During one trip she returned to her homeland and took blood samples then returned to the UK.

After isolating the source stem cells, she injected herself. In less than a year she had transitioned. Shortly afterward she met Martin.

They were lovers, kindred spirits, and soon they came up with a plan. Upon her return home she slit her father's throat in the dead of night. She had taken his gift and then took control of the operation. Changes were made as she started hiring professional mercenaries, she paid well for their services. Having learned enough about how to run things, she was able to keep the last thirty-six Hashashin alive, well fed, and drugged. They were little more than animals now. Even animals have their uses though.

Still, it was a disappointing setback when ten managed to escape. But all were eventually found and killed by her men or the Americans. Now if the plan worked, she would meet Martin in the UK and with her help he would seize control of the Circle and all its operations and assets. They would have a thousand years to decide what to do next.

She smiled again. In less than a week the ancient lair of Kazim would be destroyed, burying the secrets of the Hashashin for all eternity. Kazim and his Hashashin would be legends known for the greatest terror attack in history.

Jorgensen, her head of security, and two of his men met her at the Pleasure Palace.

"The control room is set. The transmission will broadcast in thirty-six hours. All the charges in the exit tunnels have been rigged. When the American missiles hit, they too will detonate, sealing everything. Everyone but us has cleared out." Jorgensen filled her in on the latest.

She nodded. "Very good." Then she caught a whiff of something strange. Jorgensen and his men were nervous and sweating...profusely. She smelled the fear weeping out of them.

She turned and walked closer to him. "Your final payment will be given to you when we touch down in Dubai." She had her phone in hand and showed him the amount on the screen. While he was distracted, she shot him twice in the face from her hip with her SIG. His men brought their weapons up too slowly.

The first was shot through the left eye. The other in the throat just above his body armor. She spun away as he was bringing his weapon up and squeezing the trigger on full auto, spewing a short stream of slugs. One struck her left outer thigh, while another hit her body armor, and a third blew off the top of her left ear and grazed her skull.

She woke up shortly afterward, her head splitting. The room spun when she rolled over. The three men were dead, or almost. She could smell a lot of blood, urine, and stool. It took a few minutes until she was able to sit up. Her thigh burned like fire.

She crawled over to Jorgensen. "What were you up to, Jorgy?"

She touched his face and then ran her fingers through his hair. He was still breathing, but it was only a ragged gurgle. He was in an agonal breathing pattern. Licking the blood from her fingers, then went through his pockets. His phone was locked.

She tried his fingerprint. Nope. It wouldn't open it with his face. "That isn't going to work now," she mentally shrugged.

After slipping his phone into her pocket and she checked her leg.

"It didn't look too bad" she thought as she wrapped it up tight with a piece of Jorgensens head scarf. This would have to do until she could get it properly treated. Then she used her phone camera to look at her ear. "Shit," she said, touching it gingerly.

The lobe was intact, but the top was chopped off. Then she felt the bloody crease with her fingers along the side of her head. Another couple of millimeters to the right and she would be dead.

Jorgensen breathed his last breath. She listened to his final wheeze, then wrapped her wounded head before slitting his throat and drinking deeply from the wound. After, she reloaded her SIG and limped back down the stairs.

Martin had recommended Jorgensen, said he had used him for several ops in the past. He had some explaining to do.

The Vatican

The door read serge saldino special attaché to the holy see. It was made of deep red mahogany with shiny brass fittings. It was heavy and dense and sounded good when someone knocked on it. Serge loved doors, all kinds of doors: ornate, ancient, plain, deeply carved, colorfully painted. It was his thing.

He loved to travel, always had for the last twelve hundred years. He'd visited every major metropolis in Europe, Asia, and Africa. He collected doors, and had a whole warehouse where he stored them, carefully maintained and curated them. He would give tours and show them off to other select door enthusiasts. Aside from being the special attaché to the UN for the Holy See, he was also the current "Elder" of the Circle. It was tradition that the eldest held the leadership role. The other seven Circle members ranged from nine hundred to four hundred years old and were scattered across the globe. He was excited as they all were at the news that another Born was found, a woman no less.

Their records dating back more than twelve thousand years showed that only three women had ever been found Born and joined the Circle. The rest had all been men. There were numerous women who were Made over that time but so few Born. It was possible that others may have existed, but they died or were killed before they could be found and protected by the Circle.

Even more intriguing was the Maker's spoor, verified as Kazim's. The remains of any suspected Born or Made had always been collected and preserved throughout the centuries. In this new age the remains were all carefully sampled, and DNA testing run to verify the bloodlines. His head of security had overseen the project. A technically competent man named Ellis. He found Ellis to be a little too serious at times, but he admired his work ethic.

The call yesterday was very disappointing. Lauren had not yet agreed to come and meet him. He tutted and shook his head. But he agreed with Rami that she may just need a little time to adjust to her situation. He could always fly and meet her himself, though he imagined security would have a fit if he did. And he was already having to deal with their frustration as he also planned a meeting with a Persian acquaintance in two days in Paris.

He was interested in buying a door from him. A seventeenth-century Persian lacquered door, very ornate and sky blue with a lovely patina and a complete set of fittings. It was a rare and precious thing. In forty-eight hours he expected to meet the man at his warehouse, security teams in tow of course. He could hardly wait.

Southern China

After my meditation, but before I open my eyes, I imagine how many times I have done this. How many millions and millions of times? More than ten million? Twenty million? Each time I try to find something new to see when I open them. It is a game I play to pass the time. The rest of the world comes into focus around me.

Smells always come first: sweat, old and dried. So many layers of sweat. The flaking stone in the walls. I remember when they smelled freshly cut and chiseled. I had even fashioned a few myself. The bamboo in the mats is degrading. The dregs of tea in a cup. Urine from a chamber pot in the hallway, a little spilled onto the floor when it was placed outside the door across the hall. The smell is sweet and pungent. I can smell cancer in it—colon cancer I think— and the faint hint of diabetes. I do not need to move. My nose seems to move around the room on its own. Then out the window it goes, sniffing the breeze. So many smells, I know them all well. It will rain today, very soon. A cat nearby is in season; she will be looking for a mate. A brood of baby squirrels are huddled in their nest in a tree nearby. They are going sour releasing stress hormones. Their mother has not returned to feed them, and they are dying. The pores in the leaves of the trees and bamboo exhaling their essence into the wind. A miasma of smells in swirling layers—thick and juicy, ebbing and flowing. My nose is busy sifting and sorting them all.

A gong somewhere outside in the courtyard clangs once. I shift my focus to the sounds. Practice has ended, the rhythmic grunts have ended. There is murmuring and movement. Shuffling steps in the hallway, more murmuring. I can smell my grandson Yhin, well before he arrives. The only person alive who knows my secret. There is a pause and a faint whisper. "Nǐ yǒu yīgè nǚ'ér" "You have a daughter" in Mandarin.

I open my eyes as the footsteps shuffle away. "A daughter." I smile and stand.

Beyond the stone window a sea of bamboo sways to and fro in the breeze. A line of dark clouds creeps into view along the horizon. Somewhere out there a daughter lives and breathes. I shall have to find her. Yhin will help me with that.

Portland, Maine

The plane touched down with a bounce. The engines whined as they were thrown into reverse. Two people clapped.

"Idiots," he thought. "Who claps when a plane lands?"

The half-empty plane taxied into Portland Jetport. Benton was in a foul mood. All the storm delays made for a very long wait, cutting into the safety margin in their timetable. He is the last one off and checks his phone as everyone else shuffles out. Finally, he stands and stretches, stows his phone, and leaves the aircraft. He ambles along through the security exit. He rode the escalator down; all the people waiting, hugging, and taking photos had left the area and headed toward the baggage claim. He took a sharp left back toward check-in and exited well before the baggage pickup and arrival area. A dark blue minivan pulled up immediately and he got in.

"Do we have eyes on them?" he asked the driver.

"They are inside the main house in the compound," the driver said and nodded.

"Wake me when we get to the warehouse," said Benton, closing his eyes.

Washington, DC

Rami answered the phone on the second ring. He was hoping to hear from Lauren soon.

"Yes, hello, Lauren. It is good to hear back from you. What have you decided?" Rami asked, phone to his ear. "Oh, I see, that is perfectly fine. Take some time to get your bearings. We can revisit this in a few weeks." He nodded.

"It is all right; no need to apologize. You signed for your passport so I can make arrangements whenever you would like."

"Yes, I do like to hike," He said. "This weekend? Yes, perhaps I could come up. I have never walked Knife Edge. I will let you know later, all right?"

"Very good, I shall speak to you tomorrow." After hanging up Rami frowned, knowing the Elder would be unhappy. But he was a reasonable man and very, very patient.

He dialed a number. "Hello, Your Excellency. I have unhappy news. Lauren would like to put off the visit. She is still trying to decompress and needs a little more time before she will commit to traveling there," he said, nodding.

"Of course, sir, I understand. I will check in with her in a few weeks and report back." He nodded. "And you too." Then he hung up and exhaled loudly.

Lauren was enjoying herself, just hanging out with Henri and working on the farm. The day trips into the local area were interesting and fun. It had been so long since she had that kind of relaxed fun. She had been talking about checking out some hiking trails and Henri offered to take her up to Baxter State Park to Mount Katahdin, to walk Knife Edge in a few days. Her call to Rami about going to Geneva was brief, and she inadvertently offered to have him come along. She felt bad about not going to Geneva and it sort of slipped out.

Martin was a bit vexed to find that Jorgensen had not called in to report that Su'wasee had been eliminated as planned. But his second-in-command, Decker, who was with the truck convoy, had assured him the delivery had indeed come through and that the cargo had been forwarded to their final locations. Given the increased American and Taliban activity in the area, Jorgensen may have had to hole up somewhere. Still, it was strange that he did not check in. Martin checked and was able to access the operations center in Kazim's stronghold through the satellite link and everything appeared to be in order. He and Ellis went over every detail again. Drivers in one hundred and thirty cities across the globe picked up orders for delivery.

Mountainous Region, Southern Afghanistan

In the control room a panel lit up as it was programmed to do, uploading a prerecorded video to a passing satellite, then on to numerous media outlets across the globe.

A grainy image came into focus. A cave, lit by torchlight. The camera panned right and a man appeared. The upper half of his face was covered by a Taliban scarf, only his mouth and chin was visible. He smiled, his teeth sharp and pointed like a shark's. He laughed with glee.

In broken English he said, "Kazim lives. We are coming for you. Where you live. Where you sleep. Where you worship false gods. You burn. You will burn."

He turned and placed a timer in a niche in the wall. The numbers glowing green started counting down from 12:00. The camera remained on the timer: 11:59, 11:58… After five minutes the man stepped in front of the camera again. "We are coming, and you will burn."

He put a gun under his chin and laughed as he pulled the trigger. Blood splattered on the camera lens and dripped down. He fell in a heap, only partially visible on-screen but seen twitching before lying still. The timer continued its countdown through the streaks of blood.

***

Rami left the Capitol very late. It was a long drive to Maine from DC, but the traffic was not looking bad heading north. An error message indicated a battery issue that morning and he had to send his Tesla in for service. His rental had been dropped off right on time for him to leave. He slid his overnight bag into the passenger seat and pulled out into traffic. He should arrive shortly before dawn.

***

Benton's team monitored the feed from the drones' thermal imaging. The two people in the house were on the first floor sitting facing each other. They appeared to be having an animated discussion. A third image is of the dog identified earlier, across the room on the floor by the front door. After a few hours the two people embraced, and the woman headed upstairs to the third floor, while the man remained on the first. After an hour he moved to the couch and reclined. It looked like he was watching TV.

Lima, Peru

Calví Ekkero, Special Assistant to the Deputy Minister of Dirección Nacional de Política y Estrategia (National Directorate of Politics and Strategy) and Circle member, is six hundred and thirty-nine years old. While all Circle members were considered equal, they had actual rank based on their age. It was how decisions were made. When a matter came to a vote, all ages of approving members were added up as well as dissenters. Whichever side had the most age-backed votes would determine the outcome.

Calví had spent most of his life in his home country. Rarely did he travel outside its borders. He valued his life and longevity immensely and took fewer and fewer risks as time went by. He was bitter and jaded and had an extreme dislike for Europeans in general.

He had barely survived the waves of foreigners, who had brought nothing but death, disease, and abuse to his people hundreds of years before. He worked diligently in the background, always finding ways to undermine the Catholic Church who had supplanted his people's native religion. Time had not mellowed his hatred, but he hid it well.

Standing on his rooftop garden balcony he was enjoying the sunset as the sun slipped behind Isla San Lorenzo. It had been a good day. His brief to the deputy minister was well received. He continued his work to weaken the grip of foreign powers on his country but in very subtle ways. The small policy changes and decisions his placement in the Ministry of Defense afforded him gave him a great deal of satisfaction.

Each evening, he would relive the special memories from long ago, reciting the names of his long dead beloved wives and children, saying goodbye to the day.

He poured a glass of wine grown from the small vineyard he owned that specializes in Intipalka grapes and enjoyed the bouquet. He lifted the glass to his nose and could smell the soil, and the flavor of the meager rain that fell on the grapes had imparted. He stood here in the same place as he did every morning greeting the sun and every evening as it set. The flickering flames from his barbeque grill illuminated his face. Looking down he could hear the guinea pigs shuffling around.

He had lifted the lid and picked one up, held it out to the setting sun, and slit its tiny throat. He drained the blood into a small stone bowl. The bowl had been carved by hand for him by Bachu, his favorite and most beloved among all his many wives, three hundred fifty years ago. Each was an offering to Viracocha the Sun

God, the Old Man in the Sky. He murmured prayers in his ancient tongue. The pigs were laid on the fire as well as several corn cobs.

"Eat this, Lord Sun, so that you might still remember that we remain your children," he intoned, sipping a fermented corn brew mixed with the blood.

After the sunset he remained on his rooftop terrace enjoying the city view and the wine until well after midnight. Lima was a beautiful city. The lights, the bustling traffic noises, the smells. It was like a living, breathing being.

The green timer reached 00:00. An unopened package in his apartment below began to beep softly. He was lost in thought as a strange buzzing that grew louder and louder could be heard.

Turning his head, he wondered, "A small plane perhaps?"

A high-pitched keening like twenty men screaming could then be heard. He stood quickly, scanning the night sky as a group of drones buzzed into view above his apartment building.

An object dropped at his feet as he leaped backward—it was a human skull with sharp pointy teeth. He looked up and then ran toward the stairs. The drones screamed in triumph, shouting "KAAAAZIIIIIIMMMMM!" as they swooped down and detonated, each carrying one kilo of Semtex.

The whole top floor of the building disintegrated in the blast, collapsing into two more floors below that. The ten-story building built to withstand earthquakes held up and remained standing. Glass, stone, and terra-cotta shards flew several blocks and rained down onto the streets, damaging cars and wounding the few people out walking at that hour. Windows shattered in the nearby buildings. Car alarms went off. Before long the wailing of sirens could be heard over the bedlam.

***

Rami was on Route 2 and passing through Bethel. It was after midnight. He was just accelerating around a wide turn along the river. A pickup truck was in the opposite lane, and he was momentarily blinded by the truck's lights. When his vision cleared, he saw a large snapping turtle walking across the road in his lane. Another vehicle was coming up behind the truck. He had little choice but to try to avoid it as he jerked the wheel right toward the river, then back.

He missed the turtle, but his right front wheel left the pavement and spun deeply in the softer dirt along the road's edge. He was not able to compensate and lost control, punching through the guardrail and then skidding down the slope, striking a grove of small white birch trees. The airbag hit him, and he blacked out for a moment. The vehicle came to rest halfway down the embankment amid broken trees. He was shaken up and bruised where his seat belt held him.

The turtle, an ancient female, had laid her eggs up the small slope above the road in a sandy patch of grass. She was nearly one hundred years old. Once the vehicles passed her, she untucked herself and continued across the road. Then she moved slowly down the embankment and slid quietly into the river.

Rami pushed the deflated airbag out of the way and struggled to get the driver's-side door open. He found his overnight bag on the passenger floor and pulled it out as he climbed out of the car. The glow of his taillights lit his way as he scrambled up the embankment. His face hurt and he could feel blood where the airbag had smashed his glasses against his face, cutting him. He set his bag down against the broken guard rail when he made up to the roadway, thankful to still be alive.

He opened his phone and dialed Henri, whose home was only ten miles away.

When Henri picked up, he said, anxiously, "Rami, are you almost here?"

"Henri, I have gone off the road. I just drove through Bethel and almost hit a turtle. I am fine but I almost ended up in the river. Can you come and get me?"

"Oh my god, Rami, yes of course. I will be there in fifteen minutes." Henri jumped up off the couch. He ran upstairs and woke Lauren.

After Henri hung up, Rami called AAA. A car with two young women inside pulled over when they saw him standing on the side of the road. The red glow of his taillights backlit him. One of the women called 911 to report the accident.

"Rami's been in an accident. He is nearby. I am going to go get him," Henri whispered to Lauren.

"I will come too. Is he hurt?" she asked, jumping out of bed. Napoleon was unhappy to be awakened and padded downstairs after them.

The two ran out the front door. Lauren opened the barn door while Henri went in and started the Land Rover. A call went out to the local volunteer firefighters and a county sheriff was en route.

Rick "Ricky" Williams, a twenty-four-year-old first responder, arrived on the scene, pulling up behind the women's Subaru.

"Dang, they are cute," he thought, looking at the two women, a redhead and a brunette. He sighed softly, then got out of his truck, grabbed his bag, and went to check out Rami. Aside from some bruising and facial lacerations he did not seem hurt too badly.

Two first responders arrived shortly afterward and blocked off the right lane with traffic cones. There was no traffic yet.

The sheriff arrived next and was taking Rami's information when Henri and Lauren arrived. Lauren hugged him. "I am so glad you weren't hurt. Do you need to go to the hospital to get checked out?" she said, Henri nodding in agreement.

"Yes, yes, thank you so much. The EMT suggested I get checked out, but I think that I am all right. I was not going very fast," he said.

"A tow truck is on its way here in about thirty minutes," the sheriff added.

Ricky climbed down to the car to disconnect the battery line and help prevent a fire. Both women were watching him climb down and agreed he was cute too. He was tall and thin, with a nice-looking butt in those cargo pants. As they watched him climb into the car to release the hood, a package under the spare tire of the wrecked rental car began to beep softly. Ricky reached in across the passenger seat to turn off the engine when he heard a strange sound coming from the trunk.

There was a high-pitched scream followed by "You will BURN! Long live Kaaaziiim!" Ricky and the car were vaporized in a searing blast; everyone along the roadside was knocked to the ground.

A drone high overhead monitoring on thermal captured the blast on video. "What the fuck?" Benton and his drone operator shouted in unison when the screen whited out.

***

Serge's security detail was of course having an issue with his short-notice jaunt to Paris. There was no time for much advanced work. The meeting was in an apartment near Parc André Citroën. The building was owned by the Moaddi Family's holding company. Parvis had lived in the top-floor apartment for three and a half years. Parvis Moaddi was a sixty-year-old Iranian-born French citizen. His family fled when the shah's government collapsed, bringing about the rise of the New Islamic Republic. His family were antiquities traders and considered moderately wealthy, with assets, properties, and holdings in the tens of millions.

Serge and his security detail were in two BMWs. The first car had a driver and two security men. In the second there was a driver, a two-man security detail, and Serge. The first car pulled up and the two men exited and surveyed the scene. It was a residential area: parked cars, kids playing, people walking. Once they cleared the area, the second car pulled up. Serge exited it with two more security men. The two cars remained on the street engines idling.

Serge was bracketed by the four security men. Parvis was waiting in the small garden just inside the entrance. The two men embraced, kissing each other on both cheeks and speaking in Farsi. "It is so good to see you again. I am very excited to see the door," said Serge.

"We can go right up," Parvis said with a smile.

One of the security men remained at the entrance while a second man went ahead up the circular stairs; the other two remained with Serge. Once the man reached the top floor, he cleared the area. The Serge, Pavis and the two remaining security men of them took the elevator up.

Parvis's apartment was large by Parisian standards, taking up the whole upper floor, but typical in many ways, with lofty ceilings and lots of windows and light. Most of the rooms had many objets d'art, several of which were covered with white cloths, and a few open crates here and there. Serge paused to look at a newly unpacked exquisite cobalt blue glass amphora. He recalled first seeing a similar one, if not the same one, "in a palace eight hundred or so years ago," he murmured. He had a fantastic memory and would eventually figure it out.

"It is just this way, please." Parvis motioned toward another room. The room was mostly empty, several paintings on the wall covered to protect them from the sunlight.

"Ah, there it is," Serge said, standing back. One of his guards moved to the window, checking the street below and the windows across the way from the apartment. The other remained in the doorway. Parvis pulled the cloth away to reveal the exquisite wooden door. It was in pristine condition. Robin's-egg blue, with a complex patina that develops over centuries with lacquered wood. Serge pulled on a white cotton glove to feel it. He knocked twice; the tone was nice and robust even though it was leaning against a wall. He examined the fittings, touching each…

A small device in the bottom of the amphora box began beeping softly. The guard downstairs at the entrance heard a faint buzzing sound in the street that grew louder and louder. He clicked his comms twice to indicate that he had a concern outside and for everyone to hold their positions. He stepped out and looked up in time to see twenty or so drones flying toward the apartment. The drones began to screech loudly like wounded beasts and then he heard the name "Kaaaaaaziiim!"

The guard looking out the window had seen the drones fly over the top of the building across the street. He turned and lifted Serge bodily and ran for the door. Parvis turned toward the window, unaware of the danger as the first drones slammed into the glass panes, smashing them in and followed by the rest that then detonated inside. The last thing Serge saw was the blue door and a flash of light.

Mountainous Region, Southern China

A heavy haze of incense swirled in the doorway of the temple. The monsoon had come early and drove heavy winds and rain up the valley. The bamboo forest absorbed the brunt of the wind's energy; here and there an old dead trunk would snap under the pressure with a boom like a gunshot. Ten miles from the temple, up a narrow trail that led to a hidden cave, a man trudged along. He was dressed in black and carried a large heavy backpack. For five days he tramped many miles to reach the cave. Once he arrived at the cave's entrance, he stepped inside and out of the weather, lowering his pack to the ground with a grunt. Then he went to work.

He had made the trek ten times in the last three months to place identical packs in the recesses of the tunnel. It was not his usual gig, but it paid very, very well. He carefully pulled a wooden case from each pack and laid them out on the floor. Each case contained a heavy-duty drone, which he assembled and tested, then set to take off.

Once each was in place, he opened the control panel. All ten drones showed green active lights. He armed them all in turn with a flip of a switch, set up a tripod, and attached the control panel to it. Then all he had to do was wait for the call and send them on their way. He leaned against the wall of the tunnel and waited. The wind outside started to howl.

Yhin had always had a dislike for technology, but as a Circle member he kept a small office with a satellite uplink and communication gear. He was third in line to the Elder, so he had certain duties he was obliged to perform.

Each week he would log in for updates, downloading the documents and printing them for review before burning them. He logged on now in the usual way but as the files downloaded, there was a loud *thump* on the roof, and he lost connection. He muttered to himself as he powered everything down. Then he walked outside to get a ladder to look up at the roof.

The satellite dish was on its side, having blown over in the strong winds. There was no point in trying to fix it during the storm, he thought. He was halfway across the courtyard when he heard a strange sound over the howling wind. He could make out numerous dark objects as they came buzzing over the bamboo forest into the wide clearing of the temple proper. He frowned and sprinted to the stable entrance. The stream of drones emitted a screeching whine before plowing into the rooftop over the office. He could not make it out over the wind.

Each drone detonated on impact in a series of blinding flashes and tremendous *thud*s. Yhin dove into one of the stalls as debris hit the stable walls.

Each green light on the control panel turned red one at a time. The man let out a happy sigh and nodded, then powered down the control panel. Mission accomplished. He was looking forward to his big pay day and the fun he was going to have in Thailand spending it. Unfortunately for him the control panel contained an explosive charge that detonated when the power was cut. There was a flash of light at the tunnel entrance, then a muffled *whump* followed by a small landslide covering the tunnel entrance. Wispy tendrils of smoke curled from between the rocks, which were blown away along with the hopes and dreams of the dead man in the monsoon winds.

Chapter Five

Benton, Maine

Lauren's face hurt; her ears were ringing. She rubbed her cheek and felt blood leaking from several small wounds. She sat up slowly, blinking several times. There were bright lights flashing from the police car that was on its side and which had shielded her from the direct effects of the blast. More vehicles pulled up and hands lifted her and carried her away from the flaming wreckage.

Henri grunted in pain and tried to stand. A piece of twisted metal was sticking out of his thigh. He leaned back against the Range Rover and looked around at the scene. It was horrific. The rental car was gone, and the birch trees were in flames. The two women had been thrown across the road by the blast. They were obviously dead, their car flipped over on its side. The police officer was trying to stand and was speaking into his radio. Other first responders and volunteer firefighters were pulling up in cars and trucks. It was chaos.

He did not see Lauren or Rami anywhere. He shouted their names: "LAUREN! LAUREN! RAMI!"

A woman ran up and said, "I'm an EMT, now hold still or you could bleed out." She put pressure on the wound in his leg, which was leaking a lot of blood.

Soon more ambulances and fire trucks arrived. State troopers as well. The road was blocked in both directions.

"I need to find my friends!" Henri shouted at the woman.

"It will have to wait; you will not be any good to them if you bleed out. Now hold still, I need to finish my assessment," the EMT said tersely.

Soon Henri was transferred to a gurney and wheeled toward one of several waiting ambulances. He caught sight of Lauren sitting in the back of one.

He shouted for her. "Lauren!"

She turned to look at him, holding a gauze pad to her forehead. "Henri!" She waved as he went by.

The EMT said to Henri, "She looks okay. We're all headed to Maine General in Augusta."

Lauren had only a few minor cuts on her face and a skinned knee. "Where are they taking my friend?" she asked the EMT sitting beside her.

"He's headed to Maine General. He's gonna need surgery to get that metal out of his leg," the EMT told her. "We really need to get you to the hospital and check you out too. You could have a concussion."

"No, I don't need a hospital. I've been worse off. I will be fine. Just Steri-Strip the cuts," she said.

The EMT taped the cuts closed with a disapproving look on his face. Lauren pushed her way past him out of the ambulance. "Thanks, and sorry for being a pain."

She heard a man call, "There is another one up here. He looks bad. These two are gone." She looked and could see a first responder had climbed up the embankment to check the two women and found Rami farther up. "I would call in life flight! It's bad!" he yelled.

She headed in that direction but was stopped by a state trooper. "Hold on, let them take care of him. I need your name; do you have any ID?"

She heard one trooper say, "The feds are on their way" into his radio.

She looked at the embankment, then up into the sky, and saw a drone hovering high overhead. It circled past some trees, and she lost sight of it. "I'm sorry. I—I'm Lauren Cortez. My purse is in the Rover over there." She pointed.

He took her to retrieve it, asking her if she knew any of the people alive or dead at the scene. She explained that they got a call from their friend Rami, who was on his way up to their house when he went off the road. They had driven down to pick him up. Shortly after they arrived, his car exploded. She didn't know the women but saw the first responder climb down to the car before it blew up.

She could smell familiar chemicals in the air, like what she'd smelled in Afghanistan. Explosives. "Look," she said. "I'm ex-Army. That was not a gas explosion. It was a bomb or an IED."

He nodded. "We know," he said and asked her a lot more questions.

The "Statey" said Rami was being life flighted to Maine Med, and that someone would be in touch shortly for her statement.

She climbed into the Rover and thankfully Henri had left the key in it. She drove down to Maine General following close behind the ambulance. Her mind was racing. "Who would want to blow Rami up? Why was there a drone over the scene?"

Her phone rang. It was Henri. She pushed the button on the touch screen. "Are you okay?" he asked.

"Yes, yes, just a couple cuts and scrapes. Rami is bad, they said. They're going to life flight him to Portland. Are you okay?"

"I have metal in my leg that will need to be removed; other than that, I think I will be fine. It is in the meaty part. It does not feel like it hit the bone," he said.

"Henri, that was a bomb. It was too powerful to be gasoline. I could smell the chemicals," she said, almost whispering.

Henri was quiet for a few moments. "I agree. I could smell it too after the explosion. Someone tried to kill him. But who? Why?"

A dark SUV was parked far back up the road above the crash. The two men inside talked to Benton on a cell. "The road is closed. We cannot get close enough to the scene to tell what happened or if the woman was killed," the driver said.

"The police radios said there are two women and one man dead. One woman was injured and treated at the scene. A man is being life flighted to Maine Med, another by ambulance to Maine General. There were no descriptions given. It is a forty-five-minute detour."

"Catch up to the ambulance. I will send someone to Maine Med. The state police called the feds in. This explosion looks suspiciously like a bomb. The thermal images from the drone video indicated the explosion was way too hot and energetic to be a car gas explosion. Something else is going on that we are not aware of. Get out of there now."

Locals and other traffic had been arriving a few cars at a time. People were parking on the side of the road and walking toward the scene. The state police were walking up the line indicating the road would be closed for hours. Benton told the operator, "Get that drone back in and recharged."

He called a different number and left a terse message. Some of the cars began to turn around and a few paused to ask for directions around the accident. No one noticed the SUV as it left.

Augusta Maine

The ambulance with Henri in it arrived at Maine General. Another with the injured sheriff appeared a few minutes later. Henri was whisked into the ED. He could hear the EMTs giving a report to the nurse and health care provider as he was moved into a room. A nurse followed him in, hooking him up to vitals and running a bag of saline into his IV.

"Hi, I'm Dave," the nurse said, drawing labs as he spoke.

"I need a portable for that leg," the provider called to someone as she came in. She rubbed hand sanitizer into her hands as she spoke to Henri about his medical history, asking many questions.

Lauren had pulled into the parking lot and came in through the main lobby. As she walked toward the ED waiting room, she began to pick up a lot of strange smells. Cigarettes, woodsmoke, and urine from an old man who was talking on the phone. Two young men in their twenties were watching a movie on their phone and reeked of marijuana.

An older woman had her right leg and foot bandaged; it was dirty-looking and smelled of decaying flesh. She tried not to make a face as she walked by. A middle-aged, bleary-eyed brunette with a name tag that read maria was at the desk marked receptionist, putting together clipboards for more admissions. Lauren spoke to her. "My boyfriend Henri was just brought in. Can I see him?"

Maria called out back but shook her head. Lauren was told she had to wait until they were finished with the X-ray and the doctor had left the room. So she stood off to the side.

Finally, they led her back to Henri's room.

"They are going to remove the metal. It doesn't look like it hit anything vital," Henri said as she sat down next to him.

She took his hand and squeezed it. She hadn't realized how much she had grown to care for him until that moment when relief washed over her. "I should be going into the OR in thirty minutes. Should not take long," he said, putting his hand atop hers.

"Okay. That was so scary," she said. Her ears were still ringing from the blast.

While he was in surgery, Lauren paced nervously out in the waiting room. Scrolling through her phone, she was looking for any new reports of Rami's accident when she saw several breaking news stories. Drone attacks were occurring in cities across the globe and hundreds of people were killed. "What the hell?" Her mind was racing. There was a drone over the accident scene.

One story said a witness heard screaming coming from the drones and the name "Kazim." Another ran a clip from the video sent to the world's news agencies with the timer, the crazy message, and the suicide. Within minutes it was running on every news platform.

A massive terrorist attack using drones was under way. A few of the attacks had been captured on video while they occurred. One rooftop exploding, in Lima, from a building close by. Another from an apartment building showed an attack on the Vatican. Kazim's name was everywhere.

"This cannot be a coincidence. I am attacked by Kazim's men in Afghanistan. I turned out to be Born. Rami figures out the Kazim connection. The Circle runs tests and confirms I have Kazim's DNA in my blood. Rami is nearly killed by a bomb at the same time as Kazim is sending drone bombs. Everything seems to be centered around me," she muttered, feeling sick to her stomach.

She suddenly felt very exposed and vulnerable. She looked around.

There were a few people waiting that were not here before; she had not been paying attention. One man was asleep. She had not seen him come in. She looked at the time. It was 4:00 a.m.

She got up and headed down to get some coffee at the small food court and passed someone who was not in the waiting room before. She noticed he was in his early thirties, very fit-looking, had no tats, and was wearing tactical boots. He had on a brown ball cap pulled over his eyes. He also reeked of gun oil and cordite, which meant he had fired and cleaned a weapon recently. And he had some other smell she was familiar with from the army, but she could not quite place it. His breathing was slow and deep. She paused to look out the window at the parking lot and videoed him for twenty seconds.

As she was walking back sipping her coffee she suddenly remembered. "Camo face paint!" She had always hated how it smelled. But when she returned to the waiting room with her coffee, he was gone.

She looked around, following his scent out to the main entrance. There was a security guard there. "Hey, did my friend Dave just leave? Wearing a ball cap." She pointed at her head.

He looked up when she spoke. "Uh, yeah, a guy like that just left. A blue minivan picked him up."

"Okay, thanks, that's his dad. I'll text him," she lied.

Her phone buzzed; it was a text from Henri. "I am out of the OR. It went fine. I can leave in thirty minutes. They did not even have to put me out for it. Was not as bad as it could have been," he said.

She walked quickly back to the waiting room. Henri was still in a gown sitting on the side of the bed when she got to the recovery room. His thigh had a wide bandage wrapped around it. The nurse was talking to him about hiking Katahdin while taking out his IV. She seemed to be running her hand over the scars on his forearm a little too long before she put a gauze pad and tape over the IV site. Lauren coughed and then took a sip of coffee as she walked in. The nurse stiffened for a moment, then relaxed again. She patted Henri's arm as she turned to look at Lauren.

"Hi, I'm Mandy," she said.

"Hey, Mandy, did they call you in for this?" Lauren asked.

"Yeah, but they pay me an ungodly amount for the overtime."

The woman's scent washed over her. She had a strong musky smell. She had not showered recently but there was also something else.

Mandy turned back to Henri. "Anyway, Henri. Do you have any questions about the discharge instructions?"

"No, I understand them. Thank you for the kind care." He had a bit of a grin.

"Well, I will leave you to get dressed," she said, looking over at Lauren and then back at Henri. "You can go whenever you like." She turned and said, "Have a good morning," before pulling the privacy curtain around.

I made big eyes and a big smile at Henri and whispered, "Well, she really likes you," then took another sip of coffee as he stood. I turned around while he got dressed.

"Yes, she is ovulating," he whispered over my shoulder as he pulled his pants on.

"That's what that smell is. Huh." The scent was quite distinctive.

"Anything on Rami?" he asked.

"No, I called on the way up, but they won't tell me anything unless I'm a relative," I said. "There is another thing. But I don't want to talk about it here."

"Oh, okay." He tucked his shirt in, which still smelled like the "explosion."

On the way out I pulled him into a large, handicapped bathroom and closed the door. "I think Kazim is behind the car explosion."

"What? What do you mean?"

I showed him all the news stories about Kazim and the bombings around the world. He took a few minutes to look at several of them.

"His car blew up at about the same time as these attacks happened. And I think we are being followed or watched," I said.

I told him about the man in the waiting room and the drone.

"There are no houses or businesses on that road for several miles and I noticed that drone too. It flew off shortly after the explosion," he said.

I showed him the video of the man. He watched it and said, "He looks like military. But there is a National Guard base here in Augusta up by the airport, so it is a reasonable possibility that he is just a National Guardsman. Maine has a large population of vets. One in ten adult residents are Veterans. There are a lot of retirees here. But this Kazim thing is truly strange; there is too much here to be a coincidence. Somehow you seem to be the center of a series of strange events."

I nodded. "We should head to Portland and see what we can find out about Rami." I hugged him. "I am glad your leg is better. I was really worried." He hugged me back and we left.

There were only a few vehicles in the patient visitor area. There wasn't much of a breeze and the moon was behind some clouds. Looking around, neither of us saw any minivans in the lot. Henri went to the driver's side, and I paused and started sniffing around. I caught a whiff of gun oil and cordite again. It was coming from the door handle.

"Do you smell that?" I asked him.

He took a slow deep breath. "Yeah…yeah, I do." We both looked like idiots sniffing the Rover, but then he found a magnetic disc GPS tracker under the left rear wheel hub.

"You are right, we are being tracked." He showed it to me. I snapped a photo with my phone. There was some writing and a bar code on one side. Henri frowned and tapped his palm with it, then put the tracker back.

"Let's let them keep following us for now," he said.

"Are you sure you are okay to drive." I asked

"I'm fine it was only a local and my leg doesn't hurt." he said

We got in. The smell was not inside the vehicle.

We headed down to Portland. While he drove, I looked up the device on my phone. "Looks like it's an off-the-shelf commercial tracker by LSA. It's cheap, only thirty dollars."

I updated him on the news about the terrorist attacks. There were more than one hundred reported so far. The president made a statement that the terrorists would be hunted down and would pay a heavy price. Similar statements came from numerous other world leaders. We stopped in Brunswick for coffee and bagels.

The sun was coming up when we pulled into the Maine Med parking lot. Maine Med's ED was busy too. The waiting room was packed with people. We had to wait for thirty minutes before we could talk to someone at the registration desk. They would not tell us anything about Rami's condition, only saying that he was in surgery. We could leave a message for his caregiver and when Rami was able to, he could contact us or give permission to share his information and let us visit.

Henri was livid. But we left before making a scene. "What do you want to do, wait here or get a hotel room nearby and get some rest, then check back in later on today?" I asked.

"Let's...let's just get something close by and check back in a few hours," he said, nodding in agreement. I found a nearby hotel and made a reservation on my phone.

"We will leave the Rover. I can get us an Uber." We went back to the Rover and grabbed the backpacks we packed for the hiking trip. It was only a ten-minute wait until Uber picked us up. We were in our hotel room in under thirty minutes. It was a nice room with two queen beds.

I caught a glimpse of myself in the bathroom mirror. I was covered in grime and blood. "I need a shower," I said.

Henri nodded while staring at his phone. He opened the curtains and looked out the window at Maine Med which was a few blocks away.

I took a long shower, and the hot water helped me relax. After I got out, I changed into my hiking gear, which at least was clean. My shirt and pants were torn, dirty, and had blood on them. Henri showered and changed as well. I put our dirty clothes in a plastic laundry bag the hotel provided. Then we closed the curtains and lay down to get a few hours of sleep.

We managed to get four hours of sleep before we were awakened by texts to both our phones.

The text was from an unlisted number. It read: "The Circle is broken. Go to ground and make no contact until further notice."

We both looked at each other. "What is this supposed to mean?" I asked.

"I have no idea," Henri said, getting out of bed, his brow furrowed with worry.

We turned on the news and it was wall-to-wall coverage. One hundred twenty-eight confirmed attacks. Everyone was clamoring to know who Kazim was. Initial reports were that most of the targets were mid-level government officials. Soft targets that were easy to get to. Hundreds of others were killed, while thousands more were injured. Some of the more prominent target names appeared.

Henri stood up groaning, "Oh no. Vatican official Serge Saldino, killed in Paris. He is the Circle's leader, the Elder. He was who you were supposed to meet in Geneva. See if you can find more victims' names."

We began searching the Web for more names and identified three more Circle members in less than five minutes.

"That is what this is about. Kazim's killing the Circle members, and if they targeted Rami, then the emissaries too. I cannot tell if he has targeted the members of the Ring. But he has broken the Circle and killed our leaders. That is what the text message means. We really could be in danger. If Rami had not gone off the road, he would have been at the house with us. We might have all been killed," he said.

I was trying to wrap my head around the scale of what was happening. "This kind of coordinated attack is not something you can just plan and carry out in a couple of weeks. It must have taken long-term planning and logistics. It required high levels of intelligence and coordination to hit all these people in the span of a few short hours across the entire globe. Even if you hadn't found me and learned the name Kazim, I think this was still going to happen."

Henri nodded. "We need to talk to Rami. I hope he is going to be okay" was all he said.

We headed back to the hospital and grabbed some food on the way as we walked. It was still lunchtime. There were lots of people on the street and the traffic was moving slowly. We went in through a different entrance and stopped at the hospital gift store to pick up some flowers. Henri wanted to get a card too.

No one stopped us when we went to the ICU and looked in. There were some nurses at the nurse's station, talking to a state trooper. We went in through the double door. I smiled and walked up to the counter.

"Hi, is Rami Alicide able to have visitors yet? We've been waiting since last night."

The nurse frowned and shook her head. "He is not able to have any visitors right now. He is still in critical condition. Are you family?" she asked.

"No, he does not have any living family. He is a close friend who was on his way to spend the weekend with us climbing Mount Katahdin when the accident happened" I answered.

She shook her head again. "We really cannot tell you anything if you are not family without his permission or his guardian's. I am sorry."

Henri sighed heavily. "He's my best friend. Can I just look at him through the door?"

"Again, no, I'm sorry. We have very strict rules regarding HIPAA and patient privacy. Please don't make me call security," she said.

The state trooper took a step forward and folded his arms, saying tersely, "Hey, listen, no one is talking to him until the FBI gets here and they finish talking to him. You need to move along now." He pointed toward the door.

"Can we leave these flowers for when he wakes up?" I asked.

"Yes, sure, you can leave those. I will put them in his room," the nurse said. Henri pulled out the card and wrote a brief note. I noticed it was in Arabic. He tucked it into the flowers.

"Thanks," I said.

"Okay, let's go, honey." I took Henri's hand; he squeezed mine hard, and we left.

"Well now what do we do?" I asked once we were in the hallway. "I feel like we are still in danger."

"There is somewhere we could go. It is a bit of a drive, but I do have another place in Quebec we could stay at. We could stay there awhile and see how this plays out. And I have an idea on how to lose our tail as well," he said.

"Okay, I guess so," I answered. We headed back to the Rover, which was right where we left it. We checked and did not smell "gun oil," so the tracker was probably still in place.

Gilead Maine

It took a couple of hours to get back to Gilead. Napoleon barked from the front porch when we returned. "Hello, sweet boy. Did you miss us?" I asked.

We talked in the car on the way about what to bring with us. When we arrived, Henri went to the barn and brought out a couple of milk crates full of gear. I packed a couple changes of clothes, my new passport, and some other stuff. We left the bag with our "accident" clothes on the kitchen table.

"Listen, if anything happens to me and you come back here...if trouble follows you into the house, there is another way out besides the front and back doors. In the walk-in freezer there is an exit under the pallet in the back. There is a metal door built into the floor and a ladder that leads down to a small room and a tunnel. The tunnel leads to the car barn, and it comes up behind the tool rack, or you can keep going and come out a hundred yards into the woods. There is a concealed door buried about a foot down next to a big deadfall. I have a jack under it, so all you have to do is use the jack to open it and get out and away. I keep a backpack with provisions, some money, and a handgun down there too," he said while we were in the kitchen packing food.

"Umm...okay." I nodded, wondering why he would need a bug-out bag and a way to escape if he was surrounded. He did not seem like a "prepper."

We topped up with a Bloody Mary smoothie and were out the door in thirty minutes. He left the barn for the animals propped open. But the sheep and goats were fine on their own outside. We loaded up Napoleon and his favorite chew toy. He was so excited to take a ride.

We were only an hour away from the Canadian border. The low mountains in western Maine were so beautiful. I saw my first moose; she was a big cow standing in a stream on the side of the highway munching on some kind of water plant. She paid us no mind, or any of the traffic that was passing by. "God, those things are huge," I said, my eyes wide.

"Yes, they are huge, and the males are even bigger," Henri commented.

Before long we were at the checkpoint on the border at Coburn Gore. Henri spoke in rapid French to the Canadian border guard. I only caught every third word. "Heading home to Quebec with my American girlfriend" was what I got from the conversation.

They looked at our passports and we were through in a couple of minutes. We drove on for another hour and stopped for gas in Saint-Martin. Henri pulled the tracker off and tossed it into the back of a big pulp truck full of wood chips headed to a mill I expect.

We stopped at butcher shops three times in three different towns, to pick up pig's blood. We said we were making blood sausage when one man asked what we were using it for. We got groceries and block ice too.

"So, this place where we are going was your home when you lived here during the war?" I asked.

"Yes, I come up every few years for a couple of weeks," Henri said. "I have someone who keeps the road clear and the generator in good shape."

We turned down a dirt road when we reached Saint-Gervais. It was mostly lightly wooded farm country. It looked like we were headed way out into the sticks.

We eventually pulled onto another, smaller dirt road. A long stone wall ran along it. "It sure is pretty here," I said.

Napoleon stood up and got excited. I assumed he had been here before.

"I built this wall," Henri said, "clearing the fields of stone."

The road and wall went for nearly a mile before coming to an end. There were gaps here and there where a tree had fallen over and knocked out a section. I noticed there were no power lines to be seen or even any other homes or farms nearby. But there were lots of trees and meadows.

"I own all this for about as far as you can see in any direction. It is in a family trust," he said. There was a wistful look in his eyes before they got a little misty. He looked away from me for a moment.

Butterflies and bees visited the many flowers. I rolled the window down and caught a whiff of the air. Songbirds called each other. It was quiet, sunny, and idyllic like a dream.

A large, old-looking two-story farmhouse came into view. The white paint had mostly worn off, exposing the boards now weathered gray beneath. Some of the boards looked like they had been burned, but not all the way through. The foundation of a huge barn could be seen a short distance away near a wide field, large rough-cut granite stones half hidden by wild roses and thistles. A smaller, newer-looking shed was next to the house. We parked beside it and let Napolean out.

As I got out of the car, I checked my phone and there was only one bar, if I held it up high.

"We should probably keep these off anyway," I said, powering mine down. Napoleon bounded through the grass chasing a squirrel.

"We can get the supplies in and the shutters off and open the windows to air it out before it gets dark," Henri said.

The heavy door was still solid, and the ancient-looking lock worked. Inside it was a bit musty. The living room had a huge fireplace. "You could cook a whole boar on a spit in this," I joked.

"You should have seen it blazing in the winter. It kept the whole place warm." He lit a candelabra on the mantel to give us some more light inside. Not that we really needed to see it but to make it more welcoming.

In the kitchen was a large woodburning cookstove. The flue was not connected. There was a long slate sink with a hand pump for water.

"There is a cistern under the house, but I'll have to prime this to get the pump to work," he said, moving the pump handle up and down dryly.

A cool-looking, old-timey fridge was next to the sink, the kind they had before electricity. We put the block ice in the top section and then the groceries we wanted to keep cool in the bottom door. There was a big worn-looking butcher block, a large knife and cleaver lying on top of it. A hutch held plates and glasses, and there were some cast iron pans inside the oven, a big kettle on top. Next to it was a large Dutch oven with cutlery inside it. The table was old and worn and seemed small for the space. Four chairs were upside down on top of it. We took those down and put the boxes and bags on the table.

Afterward we went outside and opened the shutters. These were the real kind of shutters—heavy, wooden, and hinged—that covered the windows and protected them from the elements.

"You built all this, didn't you?" I asked.

Henri nodded. "Yes. It took a long time by myself, but I wanted a home and a place to settle after so many years of wandering."

We got the shutters open and removed the heavy tarps he had over each window on the inside, then opened those as well. A nice breeze blew through, and there was some more light too. Napoleon barked, still chasing something through the grass.

Upstairs there was a single large bedroom and closet. The ornately carved bed frame was sturdy looking, but there was no mattress. Two large cedar trunks held bed linens and a couple of towels and some of Henri's old clothes; they all stunk of mothballs. "Yuck."

In one corner was a big wooden tub for bathing and washing clothes. There was a long, low dresser, also ornately carved. The carvings were similar to those I saw in his workshop in Maine. In the closet there were two thin mattresses rolled up and wrapped in plastic. Another wooden cabinet was in the back of the closet. I looked in it when we brought the mattresses out. There were a couple of muskets, actual Revolutionary War style muskets that fired lead balls with gunpowder. They looked well maintained and usable. There was an old wooden bow and twelve arrows in a leather quiver, and a long-bladed knife about fourteen inches in length in a scabbard. A pair of hatchets hung from a peg.

"I made those," Henri said. Then: "Do you want to sleep up here or down in the living room with me?"

"Downstairs is fine. In front of the fire would be nice," I said. It was getting dark by the time we had everything settled.

Just outside the kitchen door was an outhouse. I cleaned the spiders out and startled a small furry animal who'd made a nest there. At least there was TP in a coffee can with a plastic lid, so we weren't totally roughing it.

We lit a small fire, not that we were cold or anything; it was just comforting to have a fire. Henri made sandwiches. We drank pig's blood straight this time and chased it with bottled water. Napoleon curled up on the floor beside me while we ate.

"What do you think is going to happen, Henri?" I asked.

He was lying on his back staring up at the ceiling. "I really do not know. I am going to assume we are in danger. We do not know who is following us or why. I have been thinking about what you said earlier, about the amount of intelligence needed to locate all the Circle members and emissaries. The Circle members have security details assigned to them, like the Secret Service. We have remained hidden all this time because security is so tight and the people who run that side of the Circle's organization have been in place for a very long time. I cannot imagine how anyone could have infiltrated the organization, so that leaves only the possibility that someone high up, for some reason, betrayed us all. And it had to be someone with access to all that information. I think we should just lie low for a while. Hopefully, Rami will recover and if he is able to, then contact us. He will know where I am when he reads the card."

I lay on my back for a while, but my mind was racing so I turned onto my side and looked at him.

"I don't think I can sleep," I said. "There's too much going on in my head right now." I got up and sat by the fire, looking into it.

He sat up as well. "I cannot sleep either. I think I need to go see them. Do you want to come?"

"See who?" I asked.

"My wife and my son. They are buried nearby. I always go see them as soon as I arrive. But with you here, I decided to wait. I do not think I can," he said softly.

"Oh...okay, sure, I'll come with you," I said, slipping my shoes back on. Napoleon got up and followed us too.

There was only a sliver of moon on the horizon, but the stars and the Milky Way were ablaze. There were so many more stars, whole swathes of them I had never noticed before. With my enhanced night vision, it was like walking around in daylight.

I walked behind Henri with Napoleon trailing us. We went past the burned-out barn to a stand of trees beyond it, to a little sheltered place with a small piece of granite in the middle. I stayed back and left him to it.

He knelt by the stone and caressed it, speaking in a low murmur. I could see his shoulders start to heave as he wept. He pulled some plant growth away as he alternated between crying and talking. I teared up and sobbed quietly. I could not help myself. His pain was so palpable. I could smell the anguish seeping out of his pores. It washed over me in waves and filled the small glade, then dissipated slowly in the breeze.

Napoleon nuzzled my leg and sat down on my feet. I knelt and scratched his ears.

"Sweet boy. Good boy. Loves his ears scratched, does he not," I cooed.

Henri sat leaning forward with his forehead against the stone for a very long time. But finally, he slowly stood, picked a few errant leaves from the stone, and brushed it off again before giving it a pat. Then he looked up at the stars. I could see the tears had dried on his face, though his shirt was still wet. He wiped his face with his hands and yelled at the sky.

He turned and walked toward me across the grass, the breeze making the leaves on the trees flicker in the starlight. "Can I hug you?" I asked, almost crying again.

"I'd like that," he said. I wrapped my arms around his chest. He pulled me in hard; he was a big man, with a wide chest and huge arms. We stood there for a long time, his smell washing over me. I was getting used to it now. My body did not respond as quickly or as hard as it did when we first met. He still made my loins tingle, though. I felt warm and safe.

He gradually relaxed his tight grip, and I loosened mine. We both exhaled and stood there awkwardly for a moment. Then Napoleon squeezed between us and looked up.

As we walked back, I said, "I didn't realize I could smell emotions too."

"Yes," he said. "Our bodies react when we experience strong emotions. We do smell very differently when this happens. Trust your gut. It takes practice and experience, but you can train your nose. Sometimes the scents are very subtle. It can save your life or help you read people and their intentions."

There was a rustling noise nearby and Napoleon barked at something, then took off through the grass. "I think I can get to sleep now," Henri said, running his hands through his hair.

"Yeah, me too," I said as we walked back side by side. Napoleon came back panting.

The fire was down to embers when we finally lay down. Sleep came quickly for me, sweet dreamless sleep.

Chapter Six

Portland, Maine

"Yes, I work for the State Department as a consultant in foreign affairs. I am not permitted to say more than this. Field agents such as yourself do not have a high enough security clearance for me to be more precise." Rami answered the agent's question, his throat still sore from the breathing tube. He took a sip of ice water. He was very glad to have that out.

He cleared his throat, then said, "You've asked me this question three different ways and the answer is the same."

"We're just trying to get a clearer picture of who you are and your role in this is," the agent said.

"My role is that of a victim. I was not knowingly transporting a bomb. I had no intentions or plans to blow someone or something up. I have already explained the circumstances of my trip and why I was driving the rental car. I believe I was a target."

The agent's phone rang. He looked down at it, raised his finger, then stepped outside the room. The state trooper who was stationed outside stood in the doorway. His face flushed red, it crept up his neck and colored his cheeks. Rami knew what the man would like to do to him. He could smell the hatred seeping out of him. He maintained eye contact with the trooper and did not waver.

Soon the agent returned and spoke into the state trooper's ear. There were a lot of hand gestures from both. The trooper looked angry but deflated. They both came into the room.

The trooper removed the handcuffs from his wrist and the bed.

The agent said, "Thank you for answering my questions today, sir. Sorry for any inconvenience or distress we may have caused. Here is my card. If you think of anything else, any additional details about the event, please call me immediately." He left the card on the bedside table after tapping it twice, then set an evidence bag containing Rami's phone on top of it.

"I will," Rami said with a nod as the agent left. He turned to watch the trooper leave. Then a door could be heard slamming.

The nurses at the nurse's station looked startled and whispered to each other. One got up and came in.

"Is there anything I can get you, Mr. Alicide?" She had a small bouquet of flowers with her. He had smelled them earlier and could see them outside his room.

"Your friends dropped these off two days ago, but the police wouldn't let us bring them in. Sorry. One of them opened the card." She put the flowers on his bedside table.

"It's all right, no harm done, I'm sure." He opened the card and read Henri's note. After reading it he said, "I need to speak to the attending physician, please. And where are the rest of my things?"

Geneva Switzerland

"No confirmation yet on Yhin. Urso and Rami both survived," Martin said to Ellis.

Ellis smiled. "This is even better than we could have hoped for. Only one Circle member was left to eliminate, and the two emissaries left alive to deal with. We were more successful than we predicted."

"The woman Lauren disappeared in Canada with Henri," Martin continued, ticking through his list.

"Benton's men lost them." Ellis nodded. "She will be found eventually."

"Jorgensen has not turned up and we can't verify Su was eliminated either."

"The superpowers have located the uplink to the compound. It is time to launch the next phase." Ellis logged into the control room for the last time.

A new video was sent from the site. A gloved hand with razor blades sewn into the fingers was shown placing a timer into a niche in the wall of another dark cave. It began to count down from four hours to zero.

"Burn... You will Burn" was the only message.

A US SEAL Team inserted twelve hours prior into Afghanistan fired up a laser aimed at a heavily fortified iron door at the base of a mountain. Coordinates were sent and locked. A pair of bunker buster cruise missiles were launched from an American vessel in the Persian Gulf. Amazingly, Iran gave permission for the overflight.

Small, paneled vans across the globe, parked in industrial areas—each with a single thawed body of Hashashin inside and enough electronics to make it appear that they directed the drone attacks—suddenly burst into flames and then exploded.

Southern China

It had been a very long time since Yhin sat in a teahouse or traveled to the city. When he arrived, the owner cleared everyone out. The man who served him brought him a cell phone. Yhin made a single call, then placed the phone back on the table. The man returned with his best tea. Yhin sipped it and waited.

Four hours later a return call was made back to Yhin. An hour after that, a large Mercedes Sprinter van pulled up, its windows tinted black. Two Mercedes sedans parked alongside it. Eight men dressed in tailored business suits exited the vehicles and formed a perimeter around the shop entrance.

A ninth man exited the van and walked inside the teahouse. He had close-cropped black hair peppered with gray. It was difficult to tell his age, but he walked with a graceful fluidity of motion. Yhin stood as the man came in. A broad smile spread across his faced and his eyes twinkled as the younger man stood before him.

They embraced. "Baba," the younger man whispered.

"Shanyuan," Yhin whispered back. They spoke quietly for several minutes.

After a while the shop owner peeked through the doorway to find Yhin gone. The phone was on the table, with the SIM card removed next to the empty teacup and a large roll of yuan.

***

Tai Huen was used to the ritual, each morning rain or shine, snow or scorching heat. He and twenty other porters would rise from their cots and beds, eat breakfast, and kiss their wives and children. He would dress for the weather, which shifted at midday when the stony mountaintops heated by the sun would cause updrafts that pulled moist, hot air up from the deep valleys that surrounded the lonely peak.

His home was only one kilometer from the village. The track was a dirt one but so well packed from foot traffic as to be hard as stone. This morning was no different than the last or the one before. He arrived just before dawn. The village had grown since he was a boy.

More and more tourists came each year to walk the 12,876 steps it took to reach the peak of Mount Yiwu and drink a cup of tea that was grown and prepared by the Taoist monks in the monastery atop the mountain.

The place, the tea, and the ritual walk were considered sacred by Taoists. When he was a boy, only five porters had jobs. These belonged to certain families and were passed down from father to son.

A bus station had been built to permit more tourists, so fifteen additional porters had been added. Now small groups would come four or five times a day instead of just once or twice. It took three hours to walk up in clear weather. Each morning at 4:00 a.m. the gate to the path was opened, and he arrived ready to begin his day carrying supplies to the top.

He found a small crowd gathered around the gate. Taoist tourists were milling about, and the rest of the porters were all standing there. The supplies were still piled up in the back of the cart. Nothing had been unpacked.

"The way is closed. The way is closed," he heard someone say. He pushed through the people to the gate, which was indeed closed. The bar that one of the monks removed each morning and placed each night to open and close the way was still in position. Bits of parchment were stuck under a nail; it appeared a note had been posted and then torn away by someone. No one knew by whom. Tai was very confused and more than a little concerned.

The way to the peak had never remained closed even for a day for as long as he had been alive. People milled around for another hour before leaving. Tai too was about to leave when a procession of five monks from the temple high above could be seen trekking down the mountain. Monks never left the temple, never descended the trails, save for the one who opened and closed the way each day. When the monks reached the bottom, the porters gathered at the entrance. Surely the monks had an explanation.

Le Po, the monk who coordinated the porters, opened the entrance and stepped outside of it. He shooed away the few remaining tourists. To each porter he first bowed before placing four gold coins in their hands. This was one month's wages. He bid them return in four days.

One monk was carrying down a heavy-looking object draped in a plain brown cloth, perhaps a box. The monks then filed to the bus stop, where a large bus with tinted windows was waiting for them. It drove away into the swaying sea of green bamboo forest.

Triad Headquarters, Southern China

A long black van with tinted windows pulled up in front of a squat four-story building. There were no windows on the ground floor. The other three floors had small, tinted windows. A long, wide set of steps led to a single entrance with double metal doors. An elderly man named Hu Wei was sweeping the steps. He had been an Enforcer in the Triad in the seventies. Now in his nineties, he was still fit and clear-minded. He looked up from his task as the van doors opened. His mouth flew open as he gasped, his eyes wide with both fear and wonder. A man stepped out of the van onto the sidewalk. His entire body was tattooed from the neck down with gold and red scales. He wore a simple loincloth; his feet were bare, and his hands were empty as well. His head was covered by an ornate gilded mask, a gold-and-jewel-encrusted visage of a fearsome dragon head. The van door closed behind him and the van pulled away.

The dragon man walked slowly up the steps toward the entrance. Hu dropped his broom as the man approached. He recalled from his youth the ancient tales he was told by his grandfather about the founding of the Triad and the history of its leaders.

He instinctively dropped to one knee, whispering, "The Dragon has returned from the mountain."

One of the founders of the Triad had been called the Dragon. Hu had seen drawings of the man in his ceremonial helmet. He was a legend and highly revered.

It was said he was made of granite, could shatter rock and blend steel with a blow from his fists. No man had ever stood against him and prevailed. The Dragon man walked past him and picked up the broom. He handed it back to Hu and nodded. Four men in suits opened the doors from inside and held them wide. They bowed their heads as the Dragon man entered and pulled the doors closed behind them. Hu stood with his mouth open for several minutes before he regained his composure.

Yhin was escorted to a great hall. He was greeted by the Incense Master, the Triad's officer of all ceremonies. The man in his sixties bowed deeply to him. Yhin returned the bow, though not as low. Eight others were in the room as well. All were standing.

The Incense Master was very nervous. It was his duty to determine if this was indeed the Dragon returned. He stood before a large altar table. He snapped his fingers, and two men pushed the table to the right, revealing a niche that held inside it an ornate box covered in dust. He lifted the box from the niche and placed it upon the altar table in front of the revered ancestors.

He inspected the ancient seal to ensure it was not broken, then turned and nodded to the assembled men. Twisting the gold chain seal, the link parted. He opened the box and removed a huge tome. The book had not been disturbed or opened in centuries. Its contents and location had been kept secret, known only to him and the Mountain Master, leader of the Triads.

There was a section with a red ribbon. He opened the book, folding the ribbon out of the way. The page had a detailed drawing of the Dragon and his tattoos. He compared them to the man before him. When he was done, he turned and nodded to his leader. Then he examined the Dragon helmet; it too was an exact match. He turned and nodded again. He snapped his fingers, and a man brought forward a large wooden box, setting it upon the ground and opening the lid. Yhin said nothing. He removed the helmet, placed it in the box, and closed the lid. The man bowed and carried the box away to an antechamber.

Yhin stood calmly waiting for the next test. The Incense Master snapped his fingers and another man stepped forward. This man was known as the Red Pole, leader of the Triad's Enforcers. He removed his shirt, folded it carefully, and laid it upon the ground. He appeared to be in his fifties and was very fit. He too was tattooed from neck to wrist.

A long red staff was handed to him. He spun it, checking the weight and balance. He spun and struck Yhin in the neck, spun again and snapped rapid blows over his entire body. Yhin never moved or even flinched. He was completely still and unharmed. Red Pole felt the shock of each blow back through the wooden pole, which threatened to break in his hands. It was as if he were striking a statue. He bowed. Yhin returned the bow, though not as low.

The Mountain Master stepped forward, carrying a slab of red granite, two inches thick and highly polished. He stood in front of Yhin and held the slab of stone in front of himself. He nodded. Yhin nodded in return and moved in slow motion into a Wing Chun stance. Then he delivered a rapid six-inch punch that shattered the stone and knocked him onto his back.

Several men gasped. The Mountain Master righted himself and knelt before Yhin.

"The Dragon has returned from the Mountain," he said loudly. The men in the room all nodded and knelt as well. Yhin touched the Mountain Master on the shoulder, bidding him rise.

"I need your assistance, brother, on a matter of the greatest importance. Help me find the following people..." Yhin said.

Within forty-eight hours all the resources of the Triad and its affiliates across the globe were focused upon a single task.

Dubai

The sky was clear and moonless. The stars sparkled above as Su'wasee arrived on the northern shore of Dubai aboard a thirty-six-foot "fishing" vessel. It was well after midnight.

It had taken a week to travel overland to the coast of Iran. The boat had a low draft and was part of a network of small ships that were used to transport drugs and other contraband. The mahogany deck was covered in blood stains that had dried in the sun the previous day. Su'wasee had hired the ship and crew and disposed of them shortly after leaving port.

She gunned the twin diesel engines and the ship slid up onto the sandy beach. Then shut the engines down. Looking up and down the beach for any witnesses she slung her bag over her shoulder, then hopped over the side.

Su had been careful to avoid known contacts on her journey. She did not want Martin or Ellis to know she was still alive until she had a chance to deal with them. While she traveled, she had caught up on the news of the drone attacks, the deaths of nearly all the Circle members, and the bombing of Kazim's stronghold. The plan she helped draft seemed to have gone almost exactly as predicted.

She trudged through the fine sand and up a dune. Toward the lights of Sheikh Khalifa Hospital ahead. It took only another hour of walking until she reached the small walled compound and house she owned at the edge of the city—one of several safe houses she bought through shell companies.

After entering the security code, she opened the heavy steel door at the entrance. It protested loudly. With her foot she slid the stone she used as a door stop over the keep it open. Once inside she put her bag down and went to turn the power back on.

The hot water took a little while to heat up, so she ordered food delivery through an app.

After she ate, she showered, enjoying the hot water as it rinsed away the blood and grime from her travels. Afterward she stood drying herself in the mirror, admiring her fit and muscular body. Her ear had healed up nicely as had the bullet wound in her leg. Which was fine now, with barely even a scar.

Getting into Europe and then Geneva was going to be trickier than Dubai; it would take some careful planning. She had time and the resources to make it happen.

Four days later she got off a ferry boat in Athens with a tour group returning from Crete. She caught a cab to the train station. Two hours later she was on a train to Sofia, Bulgaria, and then on to Geneva. Thirty-six hours later she stepped off the train in Geneva.

Geneva Switzerland

Two of Martin's security details swept the apartment before he entered. "All clear," one said into the radio. Martin nodded as he walked in. "Thank you," he said curtly as they took up positions outside his door. He set his briefcase down and poured a glass of wine from the bottle on the counter. Humming a tune from his favorite jazz album he scrolled through his phone alerts as he walked into the bathroom. After a shower he shaved and dressed for bed.

Su watched him through the thermal imager.

"It would be so easy to kill him right now," she thought. "But I need answers first." She continued to watch and wait and plan.

Portland, Maine

Rami was so angry he wanted to scream. "How could this have happened? The Circle...broken?"

It was inconceivable. And yet it had happened. He could reach no one through official channels at the Circle offices in Geneva. He sent several back-channel messages to the other emissaries and received no responses. He dared not return to his offices in Washington. Whoever was behind this was well organized and had a global reach. After reading the coded message from Henri, he knew he was being surveilled and was in grave danger.

Benton had left several messages for him which he did not listen to, nor did he dare to return them. He was no longer sure he could trust the man or his team. They reported to him, but they were on retainer to the Circle.

He got up as if to relieve himself and pulled the privacy curtain across his room, then quickly removed his IV. His whole body ached as he dressed. His head was splitting. He needed blood to heal more quickly, and he needed a place to hide. His nearest safe house was in Vermont three hours away. Still, he had other contacts in Maine, in the city of Lewiston, where there was a large Somali immigrant population and a strong vibrant Muslim community. He turned his phone off. His clothes were ruined by the blast, but his travel bag, which he had brought up to the roadway, was intact.

Peering through the curtain he waited until the nurses stepped away from their station. He slipped out of ICU and made his way slowly and painfully down the bright corridor.

He paused at an intersection and checked the evacuation map on the wall near the exit, able to avoid the waiting room and lobby by following one of the evacuation routes out of the hospital.

A cab was dropping off a couple as he exited the building. He waved to the driver who pulled up.

"Do you need a lift?" the driver asked.

"Yes, please," he said, feeling winded and a little dizzy. "To the Muslim Community Center. Near Whole Foods."

"I know the place. Sure, hop in," he said. Rami slid into the back seat behind the driver. He gasped in pain and was hit with a wave of nausea.

"Jeez, are you all right?" the driver, a middle-aged man with a scruffy beard, asked.

"I will...I will be all right. I had a procedure today and the pain meds are wearing off. Take it easy on the potholes, please?" He tried to smile through the pain.

"Sure thing, man, sure thing."

It only took a few minutes to get across town. Once they reached their destination, Rami went inside. He made some calls and in two hours' time, a man arrived to drive him to Lewiston. The Somali driver said very little to him, as he'd been instructed to do.

Rami's contact met him when he arrived at Masjid Al Salaam Mosque in Lewiston, a portly man of mixed Somali descent.

"Oh my goodness, my friend. What has happened to you?" The man rushed to put an arm around Rami.

"Ah, Aaden, it is a long story, my friend. I need a large favor. One of my business interests went sour and I need to disappear for a little while. Do you still keep that camp on Sebago Lake?"

Aaden beamed. "Oh yes. I rent it out through Airbnb now. It is booked solidly through the summer, but I have another place that I recently purchased. A duplex on Long Beach."

He seemed very proud of himself. "And I have been working on it. It is almost ready to rent, but you could stay there for a little while if you need to. The interior finishes are not done yet, but it is comfortable and livable if you need it. I owe you so much for helping my father. You may use it as long as you like."

"Thank you, my friend. Only for a few days, I think. I am going to need some things too," Rami said, squeezing Aaden's hand.

"Whatever you need I will do my best to provide," Aaden said.

In two hours, he had stopped to pick up some supplies and was lying in a small travel cot in a large, empty second-floor bedroom on the beach. The space was bright and airy.

He had checked all his dressings and a few of his wounds were seeping blood. He did not want Aaden to help him change the dressings, to know the extent of his injuries. The most painful thing was where the chest tube had been placed.

He had drunk as much sheep's blood as he could hold and went to sleep. The next two days he rested and fed. While he did, he caught up on what was going on in the world.

He made some discreet searches on the new burner phone he purchased. Aaden stopped by each day to drop off supplies and had left him a car to use if he needed to go out.

By the morning of day three he was doing much better. The pain was gone, and his wounds had all closed. Other than being very stiff he felt well enough to travel.

Rami was writing a thank-you note to Aaden when he heard a knock on the door. Looking around he realized he had no weapons to speak of, just some plastic cutlery. He put the pen down. Moving quietly towards the front door he saw that Aaden had left several tool bags in the living room, so he grabbed a hammer and a razor knife. He tucked the knife into his back pocket and held the hammer behind himself as he walked to the door. He peered through one of the sidelights to see a man in a black suit. He was of Asian descent.

There was a large Mercedes van with tinted windows and New York license plates parked next to his loaner car.

"Yes. What do you want?" he called through the locked door.

"The Dragon has called you to his service," the man said, removing an envelope from his jacket pocket and putting it in the mailbox. He turned and walked back to the van.

Rami waited until the man was back in the vehicle, then opened the door and removed the envelope. He used the razor knife to open it. There was a thick vellum sheet of paper folded in three inside of it. He unfolded the sheet, which was blank. Then he smelled the paper, inhaling deeply.

Yhin's scent filled his nostrils. "Thank the gods, Yhin lives."

Quebec

We walked the fields the next day. It was like a dream, sunny and cool breezes. Wildflowers bobbed gently in the breeze as errant bees and butterflies flitted from one to another. I took Henri's hand as we walked.

"Will you tell me what happened to them?" I asked.

He did not answer right away.

"British soldiers killed them when I was away fighting," he finally said, softly. "We had just won a small battle and I was just returning when I saw smoke on the horizon. I ran as fast as I could. The barn was ablaze, and I could hear the horses' screams. They had forced my wife and son and my two young farmhands into the barn and set it on fire."

I squeezed his hand as I gasped.

He did not say anything after that for a while. Then: "I tore at the wood trying to free them, but it was too late. I was so severely burned. One of the horses kicked its way free, breaking the door and bolting across the yard. It was on fire as it ran off. I found it, days later dead in a nearby field.

"It was days before the fire subsided and I could look for their bodies," he said softly again. His eyes were teary, his cheeks wet.

"I swore vengeance as I buried them," he said, biting his lip pensively. "The soldiers had searched my house and grounds, so I was able to catch the scent of the men who did this. They were easy to track after that. There were six of them." He sighed heavily.

"In my rage I hunted and killed them all. Taking them at night and carrying them away one at a time. I brought each one back to the barn and killed them slowly, cutting them up and bleeding them out."

He looked so sad as he was telling me this. "It wasn't enough for me. I was so consumed by anger and hatred. They needed to be made to feel the terror my wife felt, so I fed on them while they were alive. The look of horror in their eyes as I drank their blood while they could do nothing was thrilling. It was a dark terrible path I went down. Before I knew it, I became a monster. What we must never allow ourselves to become.

"Once they were all dead I did not stop. I haunted the British encampments at night, taking one or two men where I could. Dragging them away into the night. I tied them to trees and did horrible things to them with my knife and teeth and left them to be found. They tried very hard to catch me but never did. This went on into the summer."

He wiped his eyes and then continued. "My mind was filled with madness by then. But as I succumbed to the bloodlust, it was making me reckless. If I could not find victims to kill, I burned supplies, stole their payroll, poisoned their horses, whatever I could think of to hurt and harry them. That summer I killed one hundred and eighty-seven men before Rami found me and stopped me.

"Many are in the fields beyond the graves. I put most of them there. I do not know what frightened the soldiers more, finding the mutilated corpses I left behind or finding their blood-soaked clothing and a few body parts."

"Oh god, Henri," Lauren gasped.

"Rami had been in the Americas documenting and investigating the various legends of the native people, in hopes of learning if our kind existed here as well. He heard of me and came to hunt down the bloody savage that was terrorizing the British.

"I had been frequently sleeping by day in the cistern under the house in between my raids. He easily tracked my scent and lay in wait. I was just returning from another raid, after I had successfully ambushed a group of four soldiers who were transporting the payroll for one of the regiments. I had been stashing the stolen gold and silver under the cistern. Some of it is still buried there.

"On my way back, I paused when I was passing the graves of my wife and son, catching a whiff of something strange in the wind. Something I had never smelled before. One of Us. It was fascinating and intoxicating. Rami was hiding nearby and shot me in the leg with a crossbow. I shouted in pain and charged in the direction from which he had fired. His next bolt hit me and struck me in the chest, and I fell. I knew my end was at hand and crawled to the grave to die with my family.

"I lay there praying to God for forgiveness. I knew I was doomed to hell." He wiped away the tears from his eyes.

"I could hear him slowly approach as I lay in the grass. I was bleeding out quickly. Then I heard his crossbow *click* as he readied the next shot to finish me…"

Suddenly, they both heard a faint buzzing that quickly grew louder.

"What's that? A motorcycle? Or a drone?" I asked him in a hushed whisper. Wiping away my tears, I had been so engrossed in Henri's tale I hadn't been paying attention to our surroundings.

"I don't know," he answered, looking concerned. We both looked around. It was late in the day and partially overcast. The leaves were rustling in the breeze and the air smelled damp, as if a storm was coming.

The buzzing grew louder somewhere to the south of us in the direction of the house; then it faded away again and finally stopped. Henri motioned me toward a stand of trees. "We should hold off going back. Napoleon, come here, boy." He slapped his leg and Napoleon padded over. His ears went down like he had done something wrong. We dropped to our knees beneath the trees and listened.

The only other sounds we heard were the rustling of leaves in the breeze.

"Do you think they found us?" I asked.

"It is possible. Tech today makes it so easy. And the Circle has the resources to find anyone eventually. This place is known only to Rami, though. He would never tell anyone about it. It may be him," he said with a worried look. "I can go in alone and make sure it is safe."

I did not answer right away. We were at least a mile from the house.

"Why not circle around to the road and see if there are any vehicles nearby. If it is a drone, the operator is usually in a vehicle monitoring it."

"Sure, makes sense," Henri agreed.

I had his big knife, and we had his bow and six arrows. He had shot a couple of rabbits for dinner. So, I carried those as well.

"There is a creek that way on the other side of those trees. A lot of brush that we can use as cover and it heads in the general direction we want to go," he said.

We moved quickly, staying as low as possible. Napoleon followed along, tail wagging at this new game. The creek was just a trickle meandering along the thirty-foot-wide gulley that was four feet deep. Henri led with me just behind. Both of us stopped regularly to sniff the air but we were upwind of the house, so that wasn't going to help. We made it to the dirt road that led to the house just as it was getting dark.

We came out of the trees across from the stone wall he built in the 1700s at the edge of his property. Checking the ground, he found a single dirt bike track in the road heading toward the house and not returning. We climbed over the wall and headed for the house.

About halfway there we heard the dirt bike coming back up from the direction of the house. It's headlight was bright and we hid behind the wall as the bike passed. The man driving it had a helmet on that looked well used and dinged up. His bike looked fairly new but was dirty and muddy as if he had been driving down the creek bed. When he finally passed us, we both inhaled deeply and caught his scent.

"Hmm..." Henri said in a low voice. "It's Jack the guy I have who watches the house and keeps the generator in good service."

The man smelled of woodsmoke and beef jerky. I could also smell cherries and cigarettes under the choking exhaust fumes of the dirt bike. He smelled of dogs and goats too.

"He wasn't due to check on the place for me till next month."

"What do you think we should do? Go and check the house or bug out?" I asked.

"He lives about two miles that way. We could walk over and talk to him at his house and find out why he came by. I wonder if Rami sent him or if Gun Oil and the drone guys did it," Henri said.

"Well, it looks like he came alone and left alone. There is only one fresh track. So, I doubt anyone is waiting at the house to jump us," I said. "I think we should check the house first. If we don't find anything then we head over to his place and find out why he was here."

Henri nodded in agreement, but he was frowning. "Okay" was all he said.

We followed the wall and headed toward the house with Napoleon. Henri covered me with his bow while I checked. Nothing looked out of place as I walked up the drive. There was a white envelope stuck in the doorjamb. I could still smell the scent of the man lingering on it.

I went in and looked around and his scent was inside as well. Nothing looked out of place, though. There was a hunting rifle, freshly cleaned and oiled, a Marlin 30-30 lever action. A box of shells was next to it as well as an old .45 Colt with another box of shells. I checked the guns and found that both were loaded. Afterward I went back out and waved Henri to the house.

He opened the envelope and pulled out a short letter written in Arabic but spelled phonetically using English letters. As he read it, he spoke.

"It is from Rami. But not in his handwriting." He smelled the paper. "It was written by Jack, the man we saw on the bike.

"Rami is safe but says we are all in danger. He asked Jack to bring the guns to us and to stay hidden and is arranging for someone to pick us up and bring us to him in Montreal. The letter ends with the word 'haboob,' a code word that means 'sandstorm' in Arabic. He and I always use one at the end of any message for security."

He frowned but nodded and handed me the letter to look at, but I neither speak nor understand Arabic. I just folded it up and put it in my pocket.

"Rami never documented this place, only that we met near here during the war. I imagine whoever is behind this will have a hard time finding us if we stay put and stay hidden," he said, thinking aloud.

"We should probably hide the Land Rover in case they look for us using drones," I said.

He nodded. We moved the car under some trees away from the house and covered it in brush. Afterward we stayed inside with no fire for the evening. I had a creeping sense of foreboding and had trouble falling asleep that night. Even Napoleon seemed restless and needed extra cuddles.

"Who is the sweetest boy?" I said, snuggling his neck.

Augusta, Maine

Earlier That Day

"I have something," Elden Boggs, aka Gun Oil, called over to Benton.

"It's about time. What do you have?" Benton asked as he got up from his chair.

"Henri made several calls this year to a burner phone in Quebec. It is not on a land line nor a cell service; this was used via Wi-Fi and I have found the IP address. I should have the physical address in a few minutes. Whoever is on the other end may know where they are," he said, feeling very pleased with himself.

Benton smiled and nodded approvingly. "Good work. Let's see if it pans out."

Not long after, Elden had more good news. "Looks like a guy who owns a farm. Here it is on the map."

Benton nodded. "Looks remote, only a few roads in that area. Hardly any structures, just fields and light forest. I will let Ellis know. He's been badgering me for an update."

Ellis picked up on the second ring. "Yes...yes...good. That is wonderful news. If you think there is a good chance, they are hiding out there, I want to be there when you capture her. I can be in the air within the hour. I will update you from the tarmac on my ETA," Ellis said and hung up. He made a few more calls before grabbing his go bag.

Quebec

Jack lived on his family farm, had done so his whole life except for a four-year stint in the army. He had never married, never gave much thought to having a wife and kids. Just him, his dogs, and his livestock. His great-grandfather had been deeded the farm by the man who owned the huge tract of land next door. The owner's family had always paid his family well to tend to the vacant house there.

He met Henri Sr. face-to-face a few times and that was fifty years ago. Henri Sr. had brought his young son up to see the house and show him around, telling him it would be his one day, that it had been in his family since before Canada became a nation. Perhaps they might be friends one day if he decided to move in and renovate. He had liked the boy immediately as they were the same age. The boy grew up and looked remarkably like his father. In fact, he was the spitting image. Jack had no idea Henri had hired a boy to play his son.

When Jack returned from dropping off the message and guns, he texted Rami, who deposited a thousand US dollars into his Venmo account. He thought the message was strange but hey—a thousand bucks for a couple of old guns he never used anymore was worth it.

***

Later that night a drone swept over the farm. It was high up, but the thermal images were clean and only showed one person in the main house and three large dogs; numerous farm animals in the barn; and no others in any of the outbuildings. Benton sat simmering for a bit as he considered what to do next. Ellis was en route and he was expecting results.

"Listen up. Prep the four-man team. We are paying a visit to this fellow named Jack to find out what he knows." Elden and the rest of the men grunted and began to pack up the gear they needed for a nighttime assault/snatch-and-grab.

Later, Ellis climbed into the panel truck that Benton and his men used as a mobile base. Benton nodded as he entered.

"We have their location, in an old farmhouse here down the end of this old road. No power or phone," Benton said, pointing at a view from a drone that was hovering high above. "There are two of them and the dog. Here, on the first floor sleeping. They do have some guns the farmer brought them, but they're only good for short range."

"Good, excellent work. The woman must be taken alive, no exceptions. ALIVE, am I clear?" Ellis made his instructions known.

"That should not be a problem. I have two teams making the approach now; the exits are covered. They will be in position shortly. One group will insert flash-bangs through these windows and the other team will enter through the kitchen door near the outhouse. They will use Tasers if possible and nonlethal tactics to restrain the girl. The man they will kill with small-arms fire." Benton showed him the locations.

"The three of us will be a short distance away in the pickup vehicle. We will move the restrained woman to this vehicle and then leave. My men will clean up after we are gone. It is an hour back to the city and then the airport. Wheels up in under two hours," Benton said.

It was a good solid plan. A simple one, but that was how he liked to operate. Too many steps lead to too many chances for error.

"Sounds like an excellent plan," Ellis said, grinning. He was so close to his goal he could taste it, sweet and satisfying like fresh warm blood.

Chapter Seven

Quebec

T-minus 4 Minutes

The night was cool, clear, and breezy as the two four-man teams approached and got into position. The pickup vehicle rolled to a stop a hundred yards from the house along the stone wall Henri had built.

T-minus 3 minutes

The Mercedes panel truck parked at Jack's farm sat in the driveway, engine running. Mason Dee had been a drone operator for the USAF for four years before he got out and was recruited by Benton. He enjoyed the work even more so now in this job, and he was paid ten times what he got as an E5.

He continually scanned Henri's home. There were two figures a few feet apart reclining on the floor with a dog between them.

The assault teams called in that they were in position and Benton responded, "We are in position as well."

The drone operator said, "No movement. All clear."

"T and go" Benton said into his comm.

Team One tossed two flash-bangs through the front windows as Team Two's breacher shouted, "Breach, breach, breach!" Team Two's breacher hit the kitchen door with his hand ram, and it bounced off. Henri had crafted thick, heavy hardwood doors when he built the home. The breacher hit the door again and it began to give a little; the third strike broke the hasp, but the door only moved an inch. A large object: the antique fridge was blocking the way. As he swore and heaved against the door, Team One began its entry out front with similar results; this time, it was the huge maple chopping block wedged against the door.

Shots rang out from the windows above as Lauren fired the Colt at Team One below, winging the grenadier at the rear, hitting him in the shoulder and on his helmet. The .45 slug hit hard enough to rattle his brains for a moment and he fell back before he was able to lob the tear gas grenade, he was getting ready to toss in. Henri rapidly fired the 30-30, levering shell after shell at Team Two. He forced the other two behind the breacher to scatter.

T-minus 15 minutes

Mason was wearing a headset and didn't hear the van's door open, but he did feel the van shift as someone stepped inside. He turned to look as a masked assailant fired twice with a silenced pistol. The light from the flashes illuminated the darkened van for a brief moment. Two more masked men entered the van, and one took Mason's headset. He began operating the controls.

T-minus 3 minutes

It was Lauren's turn to be on watch while Henri and Napoleon slept. The breeze was heavy with so many scents, a wide variety of wildflowers that also carried the men's scents through the open window. She smelled the men and their gear as they approached the house well before they arrived.

"Henri, they are right outside," she said in a hushed tone. Henri opened his eyes and scooped up Napoleon.

"Upstairs then," he said as he grabbed the rifle and the two moved quickly upstairs. They slid the heavy bed frame over the opening, then each moved to either side of the window to see who was coming for them.

"T and go"

Both Lauren and Henri heard the glass break below followed by loud *whump*s! The blinding light flash was so intense it penetrated the cracks in the floor, hurting their sensitive eyes and catching them off guard—but only for a few moments. Napoleon barked and whined as both the downstairs doors began to crash inward. Henri and Lauren opened fire.

"We're taking fire, we're taking fire!" was heard over the comms. Benton watched from the front seat of the pickup vehicle, a large Rivian R1S. He had selected it as his choice due to the cargo space size and silent EV motor. He found this type of technology extremely useful for this type of covert op.

He was shocked to hear the dialogue from his teams and see they were under fire from the second floor when Mason indicated that the drone thermals showed no movement from the sleeping figures downstairs.

"Pull back! Pull back!" he shouted as he drew his sidearm and exited the vehicle to back up his men.

"Wait here," he told Elden, aka Gun Oil, who was driving. Ellis began to swear angrily and demand to know what the hell was going on. But Benton did not reply as he slammed the door. He raised his gun to fire at the second-floor window to provide cover fire, but a huge spotlight switched on from a helicopter above, blinding him.

Ellis could not believe his eyes as Benton began to twitch and dance. His arms were thrown wide before he slumped to the ground as an automatic weapon fired from above. He was even more shocked when the weapon stitched bullets across the hood and roof of the vehicle. Bullet holes appeared in his legs and torso as he was slammed back into his seat. His hopes and dreams and all his grand schemes oozed away with his blood and pooled into the carpeting, which still had that new car smell.

Recognizing the incoming .50-cal fire, Elden managed to fling open his door and dive out onto the ground, rolling to the wall and seeking cover behind the heavy stones.

The gunner leaning out of the helicopter killed the two Team Two members just as the breacher forced his way into the living room. His Taser was not going to be of much use, so he pulled his sidearm and began randomly firing through the floor upstairs. The copter circled around to the other side of the house. The grenadier in Team Two tossed a tear gas grenade through the second-floor window; it landed near the stairs and began to quickly fill the room with gas. Henri got a face full as he turned and began to immediately tear up while gagging and coughing. Lauren held her breath as she grabbed one of the heavy curtains and shoved Henri toward the closet, pushing him in and shooing Napoleon inside as well. She pulled the door closed behind her. She stuffed the curtain along the base to keep the gas out as she began to wheeze and cough.

The three men downstairs could not raise Benton or Mason to get a sitrep, after hearing Benton's order to pull out. The copter gunner strafed the kitchen entrance as it swung around.

"Fuck! Fuck! Fuck! This was supposed to be an easy subdue, snatch-and-grab!" one of the men shouted.

"Benton fucked up! I did not sign up for this! We have lost half the team!" the breacher from Team Two said.

"We don't have the weaponry to handle a helicopter with a .50 cal," said the breacher from Team One. "We can surrender and hope they don't kill us, or we can split up and make a break for it when the copter passes around again."

After a few moments of deliberation, the two exited the front of the house, hands raised, and knelt on the ground while the third man ran out the back.

Henri sputtered and fumed as the tear gas burned his eyes. Lauren reloaded the Colt as Napoleon whimpered and huddled in the corner of the closet. A short while later the gunfire stopped. They could hear a helicopter landing in the driveway.

"Henri! Lauren! Henri! Lauren, it's me, Rami. Are you injured?" Rami's familiar voice was calling up the stairs they had blocked. Lauren cracked the door; the tear gas had mostly cleared from the cross breeze of the window, but the air still stung the corners of her eyes and nose. Having enhanced senses had its drawbacks.

"We are alive! We are alive. We are okay, Rami," she called down. The two moved the bed frame and embraced on the stairs.

"Thank God you came. I was not sure we could take them," Henri said. Napoleon ran down the stairs and outside.

"Come. Yhin's men will take care of this mess. I have a helicopter waiting." Rami ushered them out through the carnage, his hand firmly on Henri's shoulder.

An Asian man in camo gear walked toward them from the wrecked SUV.

He spoke quickly and tersely. "We have two who have fled on foot. We will run them down before they reach the roadway. The passenger in the back was identified as Ellis Brugues, security chief of your organization." Yi handed Rami Ellis's personal effects: wallet, passport, a small leather valise.

"His phone was in his shirt pocket and was hit by a bullet," the man continued.

Rami stiffened when he heard this news. Henri looked grim as well.

"Thank you, Commander Yi." Rami nodded and turned to Lauren and Henri. "We should go. We can talk more on the chopper."

As the three climbed aboard. Lauren called Napoleon. "Come on sweet boy. Come on." Once they strapped in, Napoleon jumped into her lap.

"You were such a good boy, so brave." She scratched his ear as they lifted off.

"So, it was Ellis Brugues then," Henri said.

"Yes, it had to be an inside job to have killed so many and be so precisely timed," Rami answered.

"Who was this guy?" Lauren asked.

"He and his brother Martin were Made at the end of World War One by their father, who was Born and worked in our organization in the intelligence wing. He was a good man, but he was killed at the beginning of World War Two. Ellis has been the security chief for fifteen years. Martin heads up the science division, handles all our genetic research. Serge Saldino was very interested in genetics, and he had Martin trying to find ways to track bloodlines and predetermine who might become one of us."

"Were they in this together?" Lauren asked.

"I assume so. I have known them for a long time, and they have always been thick as thieves," Rami said.

"Where are we going?" Henri asked.

"I need to get you two to safety and then I need to get to Geneva. With Ellis eliminated the threat is lessened. Our offices are on lockdown but with Ellis's credentials in hand I can get in now."

"I hope you do not think you are going in alone. I am coming with you," Henri said, putting a hand on his friend's forearm.

"Me too, Rami. Me too," Lauren added.

Rami shook his head. "Yhin has provided me with a security team. I hate to put you in further danger. You, Lauren, are the future of our order. We need to keep you safe."

Lauren took his hand and said, "I want in. I have felt afraid and out of control since this whole thing started. I need to take back control of my life and destiny. Besides, I was invited by you and Serge to go to Geneva."

"All right, all right, you can come. You both can come," Rami said finally, and smiled wryly.

"So Yhin lives. Then the Circle is not broken." Henri nodded.

"And possibly Urso, my Asian counterpart. I have not been able to make contact with him. He is a bit of a stickler for protocol, so he may not respond until he receives confirmation that it is safe to do so," Rami explained. "We will be at the airport shortly. Yhin will have already received a report from Commander Yi."

"Who is Yi?" Lauren asked.

"A Red Army commander now on the payroll of the Triad. It is complicated, but Yhin made it happen," Rami answered.

"Yhin has Triad connections?" Henri asked.

"He was a founding member," Rami said, scratching his nose.

"Really?" Henri looked impressed. He had heard some legends about Yhin being a Chinese warlord that at some point took up being a monk living in a remote monastery.

"When this business is dealt with, we will convene a conclave and choose new leaders for the Circle," Rami answered.

Once they arrived at the airport, Rami spoke to Yhin for a half hour while Lauren and Henri waited.

Rami briefed them afterward. "All right, Yhin has agreed with my assessment. A security detail will be awaiting us in Geneva. They will have located Martin by then and we will find and apprehend him for questioning. Yhin will not be joining us as the only living Circle member; he must be protected at all costs until the new members are seated. The plane is ready, and we should depart."

Rami turned to look at the dog. "As for Napoleon, I have arranged for someone to take care of him until we return stateside." Everyone turned and looked at the dog and his tail started thumping the ground.

After the adrenaline wore off, they slept for most of the seven-and-a-half-hour flight, arriving in Geneva at 8:00 p.m. local time and awakening bleary-eyed when they touched down.

***

Martin paced his office. It was overcast and raining in Geneva. He was beside himself with worry. Ellis never missed a call-in and now he was four hours overdue. The plane was still waiting for him at the airport in Quebec. He called the number again and it went straight to voicemail.

"Did the mission fail? Had he not apprehended the girl?" Benton's team was top-notch. It was inconceivable that something happened to him. That he failed somehow. He had contacted Ellis's security detail in Quebec, who reported back that Ellis had not returned from his "important private meeting."

They were still angry that he had excluded them and gone alone. Martin gave them the meeting location.

"Go search the area and let me know what happened," he told them. That was two hours ago, and they had not reported anything back. Nor did they answer his calls.

"Okay. Think, think, think." He tapped his forehead. "What would Father do?"

"Hope for the best but plan for the worst," he finally said aloud. He began to back up all his work and data to his remote off-site server.

"Without Ellis there is no way I can make this plan work," he muttered while checking the balance of their accounts. They had siphoned off $124,000,000 in operating funds to thirteen different accounts. It would be easy to disappear and hide out a long time with that kind of money. Martin walked back through the empty office area. Main power was out and only the emergency lights were on. A red light was flashing on the elevator panel. The security systems had every door locked down. He swiped his card to bring the elevator up so that he could head down to the server room.

While he rode down, he listened to the elevator music and went over his escape plan in his head. He had several aliases that Ellis had created for him, including the one he used when he met Su. He felt a small amount of regret having her killed as he had started to have real feelings for her. He'd even imagined several futures they could have lived in the centuries to come. But Ellis did not want any loose ends and he had never really trusted her anyway. After all, she did murder her own father and took over his empire. She was ruthless but had a hard kind of beauty. And the sex. He shook his head.

"My god, the sex." He imagined how she smelled and felt and tasted. He had known many women and never had his breath taken away before, not like he did with her. Probably he'd never find another one like her, even in a thousand years.

The elevator stopped and the doors began to open. He looked up to see it was the wrong floor. Terror stabbed through him to the core.

"Grab him!" Rami commanded as two large men rushed into the elevator and pinned him to the wall.

"Wait! S-s-stop!" He wiggled his chin around and got out a strangled squeal.

"Oh, thank God you're alive, Rami!" he sputtered, struggling to speak with an arm wedged under his chin and practically lifting him off his feet.

Rami stepped in, his normally dark smiling eyes now filled with hate and contempt. Martin could see his security team dead on the floor beyond the elevator where Lauren and Henri were tending to two injured men. Rami turned and noted the button Martin had pushed.

"Ah, the server floor. Going down to hide yours and Ellis's tracks? Well, let us go down and see what you two have been up to." As the doors closed behind them, Lauren and Henri heard Martin start to scream.

After thirty minutes the security lockout was disabled, and the emergency lighting clicked off as the normal lights came back on.

"Uggg." Lauren blinked in the bright fluorescent light.

"There, that should hold you for a bit," she said as she finished wrapping up the man's wounded arm.

"Thank you," he said. She looked over at Henri, who was shaking his head. He laid the man's arm over his chest and closed the man's eyes. The lockouts on the doors and elevators went from red to green.

The elevator started to come up from the sub-basement server room. The doors opened and Rami waved them in.

"Come. Come. Martin has been most forthcoming about his plot. You will want to hear this."

Martin was crumpled in the corner with the two men standing over him. They could not see his face, as his curly red hair blocked their view. He was otherwise a bit disheveled but not bloodied.

"It doesn't look like it took much to make him talk," Lauren said.

Henri laughed. "You've no idea how persuasive Rami can be."

Rami only smiled grimly; the silence on the trip up was punctuated by deep sighs from Martin. He was dragged into Ellis's corner office and shoved roughly into a chair.

"Please, please, I'll tell you anything you want," Martin said, completely deflated. Henri leaned against the doorway. Lauren stood in the middle of the room, arms crossed, almost to the point of hugging herself.

The two security men left the room and waited in the hallway as Rami sat on the corner of the desk.

"You've given me the short version. Now I want the whole story from the beginning and leave no detail out."

"I can't believe Ellis is dead." Martin shook his head and rubbed his eyes.

"As long as you cooperate you won't have to join him." Rami said nodded.

***

Su had been on her perch all day, ever since Martin arrived.

"That changed things." she said as she watched the four of them through the scope of her rifle. She kept Martin in her crosshairs. He was clearly disheveled and under duress. While she had no listening device in the room, she was an accomplished lip-reader. She got most of what was being said from Martin, but the others were facing the wrong way. This new development was intriguing.

"Ellis, dead?"

Martin was going over the genetics program, tracking bloodlines to monitor who might become Born and then on to the real possibility of a central being, an "Eve" who had existed for at least twenty thousand years, and who last had a child in France in the 1700s. In fact, she had children all over Europe, Africa, and Asia the entire time. While he had confirmed several bloodlines in the Americas, Martin was certain that one or more of Eve's descendants traveled there but not her. The models, sampling, and extrapolation estimated over one thousand children survived birth and had at least one child to pass the gene to. He had now confirmed over six hundred primary bloodlines, thousands and thousands of secondary, meaning that there were now hundreds of thousands of carriers of the gene that caused one to become Born. Fortunately, it very rarely became active, though the chances increased if bloodlines crossed.

He pointed out that Lauren was a cross of four such bloodlines. She was a missing piece of the puzzle.

"Hers is currently the most potent bloodline. No other Born has more than two bloodlines. Those with more factors like this tend to live longer, be more vigorous, and heal faster than those that do not. I estimate that Lauren should be a very potent Maker. Her Made will live longer than most of the others and even some of the one or two lines Born."

Su already knew all these things. Her medical genetics background had been key to Martin's research development.

"Since we cannot locate Eve, we had hoped to obtain a larger sample from Lauren and culture it, possibly doubling our life spans. If we harvested her eggs and fertilized them with a double bloodline, we might have been able to grow a six-bloodline embryo that we could have harvested stem cells from."

"Jesus Christ!" Lauren muttered in disgust, putting her hand defensively over her belly.

"Allah Yakhthek!" Rami swore at Martin, shaking his head. All three glanced over at Lauren. Henri wanted to snap the man's neck with his bare hands.

"If we could have tweaked the gene, we might be able to get even closer to Eve's original gene. Su was fairly certain she could—"

"Su? Who is that?" Rami asked, raising a hand and interrupting him.

***

When Martin said her name, Su pulled the trigger of her .50-caliber sniper rifle. The windows of the building offices, while bulletproof, were only the standard level for small arms. It barely even slowed the round down. Martin's head exploded before he could answer. The round passed through the wall into the offices beyond. His chair spun around, dumping his lifeless corpse onto the floor.

She calmly laid the gun in its case. Then she hit a timer that would detonate a thermite charge, destroying it and setting fire to the rooftop utility room in which she was camped out. She had already prepped the space and disabled the sprinkler system in the room. Due to the intense heat, there would not be any DNA to trace.

She hit the basement button and rode the elevator down, contemplating her next move.

The elevator stopped on the ground floor and a well-dressed elderly man nodded at her as he walked in. She smiled broadly, then quickly checked that no one else was coming. The man pushed the button for the third floor. He was going up, not down. As the doors closed, she sighed. She really hated when people pushed both buttons rather than only the one in the direction they were going. She shot him in the head with her silenced SIG.

"You might still be alive if you had been more thoughtful..." she muttered. He had seen her face anyway.

When the door opened in the basement, she dragged his corpse to the trash room and left him on the floor, closing the metal door as she left. As she exited into the alley beyond, she pulled the fire alarm to provide additional cover.

The night air was cool as it stroked her cheek. She pulled up her collar and walked to her safe house nearby. Her route avoided any obvious cameras.

***

"Su? Who is that?" Rami asked, raising a hand and interrupting him. Lauren saw a flash in the corner of her eye from the rooftop of an adjacent building when Martin's head exploded.

"Sniper!" She dove for cover against the wall.

Henri scrambled back into the hallway, shouting, "Stay down! Stay down!"

Rami dove behind the desk, swearing in Arabic and crawling for cover. His face and chest were covered in bloody chunks. Everyone was quiet for a few moments waiting for the next shot to come. Ten seconds passed.

Lauren whispered, "I saw a flash across the street..." She did not know why she was whispering.

Rami wiped his face with his hand and flung off bloody residue, sputtering, "Guhhh..."

Henri killed the lights in the hallway but dared not reach in to turn off the office lights. Everyone stayed low and quiet, but no further shots came. Lauren moved along the wall toward the other window while Henri peered around the doorframe. "There is a fire on the roof of the building across the way," he said.

"Does it look like the shot came from that direction?" Rami asked.

Lauren looked at the hole in the window and the wall and the location of Martin's chair. "It definitely came from that direction," she said, scooting across the floor and reaching up to kill the lights.

Henri grabbed her wrist before she could and pulled her through the doorway. Once she was clear, Rami bolted from his spot and through the door.

"We need to move out of this area," he said to her.

"I know," she said.

Rami took off his shirt and wadded it up, wiping his face. "You two report to Commander Yi and check on your men," he said to Yi's two security men in the hallway before heading towards the men's room. "I need to speak to Yhin."

Once inside he washed his face and hands. Lauren and Henri followed him in. "This is all so crazy. What they were going to do to me," Lauren said.

"Su. Who the hell is she?" Henri asked.

"No one in our organization with that name or code name," Rami answered. Once he was clean, he discarded his bloody shirt in the trash can.

"Once we reestablish contact with our agents and the Ring, they can run her down. Yhin may have the Triad assist as well, I am sure. Come, I have clean clothes in my office downstairs. And I could use a drink."

He unlocked the door and went inside, leaving the lights off. He had a nice office, with lots of mementos and relics from across the ages. A crossbow hung on one wall. A section of wood that was ornately carved on another. There were photos of him in various locations around the world. In the window was a small orange tree. He walked across the room and looked down below. Then he touched the leaves and fruit. "This is from my family's orchard. It still exists today, owned by a very nice British family."

Light could be seen outside from below as the fire department and police trucks arrived, converging on the building where the shooter fired from just up the street. Rami did not linger in front of the window. He dialed a number on his cell and put it on speaker.

"Hello, Rami." Yhin's voice was so serene sounding, a chill went down Lauren's spine when he spoke.

Rami responded, "Yhin, I am here with Lauren and Henri. The mission was mostly successful. The building is secure, and our systems are now unlocked."

"Excellent news," Yhin said.

Rami continued. "I briefly interrogated Martin and have an understanding of what they were up to, but a third party shot him before a more detailed interrogation could be completed."

"A third party?" Yhin asked.

"Yes, it is unclear who the shooter was, but Martin admitted to working with someone—a woman named Su—on his genetics program."

There was a long pause; then Yhin replied, "You've done excellent work. We need to begin establishing contact with our people.

Also, I have bad news. It was just confirmed that Urso was killed after all. You are my only emissary left. I want you to take charge of the operations there. Lauren must be kept safe until this third party is identified and found. I would like to have her brought to my monastery for protection. I would like to meet her and have something important I wish to discuss with her in person. Henri may accompany her as well."

"I...uh, okay. Yes, I will agree to that," Lauren said, her eyebrows pinched together and looking a little worried about her situation.

"Yes, of course," Henri agreed.

Yhin paused for a moment before continuing. "Excellent. Commander Yi will make the arrangements and handle the transport."

Rami nodded. "I will begin making contact with the Ring then, Sir. I will report back our progress."

"Very good. Goodbye."

As Rami hung up, he said, "Damn, Urso was a good man. He survived in Russia for over four hundred years through all the upheavals, purges, and wars. He will be missed." Lauren put her hand on his shoulder.

"Come with me. We have much to do," Rami said, looking up.

Chapter Eight

"I was shocked at how many Born and Made there are in the world," Lauren said to Rami after they finished the notifications to everyone.

"Things will return to normal very soon," he told her. Henri nodded in agreement. "But fourteen hundred eighty-six out of more than seven billion? Not really a lot."

"I guess you are right. I am just glad we are done with the phone calls," Lauren said.

It took forty-eight hours to contact everyone. Much of it was done electronically through some means, either by text or email, but quite a few needed to be called directly. A code word was given and in some cases a code word was received back. There were lots of questions and concerns raised that Lauren had no answers for. All she could say was that their "new emissary would be in contact at some point." After six hours the assistant security chief came in and met with Rami for two hours. After thirty-six hours personnel began trickling in. So many different nationalities, it felt like it was the UN. Lauren thought it might be wonderful to work here with the rest and get to know more about their strange existence. Especially after meeting a gorgeous Spanish guy who smelled so delicious, she broke out into a cold sweat and almost tore off her clothes in front of him...twice. And that accent made her knees weak. He was an incorrigible flirt, which only made it worse.

A few of the women there warned her off him. He was more trouble than he was worth, but damn he was fine.

***

We heard that there was an arson attack across the street and that an old man was murdered by an unknown assailant. Commander Yi arranged for their transportation: an armored car with two other chase vehicles. Lauren felt like she was an important dignitary with her own big motorcade. The trip to the airport was uneventful; thank goodness they boarded a flight out on a private jet.

It was just Henri and Lauren in the passenger cabin. The flight attendant only came back a few times to check on them and bring food. The flight wasn't bad, but it was long, almost eleven hours in total.

They landed in Yunnan Province, in the city of Kunming, feeling well-fed and rested. Lauren had never heard of it. Afghanistan was the furthest east she'd ever been.

They were traveling under different names on business as employees of a Chinese casino in Laos. Customs was a breeze. Neither of them spoke any Mandarin, so they thought they would be at a loss most of the time. But in the end, everyone they met spoke excellent English. Lauren decided she was going to have to learn a few more languages and since she had the time she would.

Three Mercedes Vans were waiting for them at the airport to take them to Yhin's monastery. Security was tight and professional. It was a good mix of men and women all in identical suits and shades. They felt safe. The drive, on the other hand, was six hours long.

The views were spectacular once they left the city. They entered a beautiful region in the foothills of the Himalayas: a vast forest, a huge sea of bamboo. It was stunning. Passing through a small village, they turned up a long narrow dirt road and after nearly an hour came to a stop. In a clearing ahead was a huge stone monastery. Ranks of men and women were performing their katas in the courtyard.

The security team let them disembark. They thanked them and walked toward the courtyard. The bamboo forest did not reach all the way to the walls; there was a wide area with rows of gnarled and deformed trees.

A few of the monks were striking the tree trunks with their fingers, which looked terribly painful. There were finger- and hand-shaped dents in nearly every surface of the trunks for about four to five feet up, an inch deep in places.

A smiling monk was waiting for them at the entrance. He was Chinese but spoke English with a British accent. "Good day to you both. I hope your trip was safe and enjoyable."

"Yes, it was, thank you," Lauren answered. Henri nodded in agreement as he watched the monks and looked around at the buildings.

"If you please follow me. Yhin will not be able to meet with you this evening. He has been delayed unfortunately," he said.

"I'm sure he has a lot on his plate right now," Lauren said, looking around.

"It looks like something out of a movie," she thought. They walked around the edge of the main courtyard into a much smaller one. A stable was to the right, across from which there was an ornate temple with an attached wooden building that looked like a bomb had gone off in it. Most of the debris had been cleared away. A few small carts sat nearby with tools in them.

They entered the temple. There were tall pillars. Gold and red seemed to be the main color scheme, and incense was burning. Lauren had a burning question to ask the monk.

"Please excuse my ignorance but what kind of temple is this? It is very pretty," she said.

"It is Taoist," he answered, nodding. "We seek immortality through the cultivation of the mind and body."

That raised Lauren's eyebrows a little. Neither she nor Henri had smelled any Born or Made nearby, at least none that had recently been here. Lauren didn't want to ask Henri if he smelled anything in front of the man.

"May I be indelicate and ask what your sleeping arrangements might be? I was asked to prepare two rooms but if you are together, I can easily accommodate that," he said without looking up.

"Oh, um…we aren't a couple, just friends. Two rooms are fine," I answered.

"I must also apologize that our accommodations are very 'rustic.' The rooms are simple and not very comfortable if you are not used to such a lifestyle," he said, nodding.

Henri said, "We'll be fine, I'm sure."

They turned up a back hallway onto a stone staircase. The walls were rough hand-hewn stone.

"You both are across from each other here at the top of the stairs." The monk opened a door to a small room, little more than an alcove. "Rustic" was an exaggeration. At least in Lauren's mind.

"The sleeping mat is rolled up there. A chamber pot is by the door. Keep the lid on and leave it in the hallway if you use it. We do have toilet paper, now!" He seemed excited by this. Then he pointed out a small wooden table with a wooden bowl and a clay pitcher full of water on top. Next to that was a tall, fat candle on a plate. There was one small window with a wooden shutter to close it.

"At the other end of the hallway and down those stairs will take you to the hall where we eat. There is usually something there if you get hungry or thirsty. You are free to walk around inside the grounds. We have several lovely gardens. Please do not speak loudly or you will interrupt prayers. If a door is closed, please do not open it. Doors are typically closed during meditation. Now, I have other duties to attend to. Yhin will send for you when he returns." He bowed and walked down the corridor to the hall below.

Lauren and Henri both looked in the rooms together. "I've had worse accommodations in the army." Lauren said.

"As have I," Henri agreed, though he did not look pleased to sleep on woven mats. But when in Rome...

"Fancy a walk?" Lauren asked.

"Sure," Henri said.

They walked back outside and followed their noses to one of the gardens, which was full of exotic flowers and delicious scents that tantalized the nose. No one was there and they did not know the names of any of the flowers, so for fun they started giving them silly names. This kept them entertained for nearly an hour.

Suddenly Henri stiffened, his nose in the air. "Do you smell that?"

Lauren walked toward him, then caught a fleeting whiff of a new smell. She could tell it was a woman. The scent was more potent than any of the Made or Born that she'd gotten used to smelling so far. So many subtle layers to it; comparing them was like comparing candlelight to sunshine. Then it was gone.

"It is a Born woman," Henri said, his voice quivering and wistful. "I have only ever smelled two Born women now. You and her. Her scent is so strong."

"I thought there weren't any Born women but me, Henri. There wasn't anyone on the list and none here," Lauren said. "Has Yhin got one stashed somewhere that no one knows about?"

"Perhaps she chose not to join the Ring and Yhin honored her request," he said thoughtfully.

"I suppose. I wonder if this has something to do with what he wanted to talk to me about." Lauren was puzzled.

"Henri, we have been sitting for days. I feel like running. Care to join me?" she asked.

"No, I think I will explore the other gardens," he said, shaking his head.

"See you in a little bit then." Lauren headed back to her "room" and changed into shorts and a T-shirt.

The courtyard was wide and currently empty, so she began to run laps around it. Her breathing was good, as her limbs warmed up. She felt like she could run forever. The sun was getting low when she finally stopped and walked a few more laps.

She checked her pulse at her neck and noticed a figure as she looked back up. A woman was standing at the entrance to the flower garden where she and Henri had just spent time. The woman beckoned Lauren to follow her, then stepped back into the garden. Lauren looked around and the courtyard was deserted. The armed guards just outside of the gate were the only people she saw. She walked after the woman, fanning her T-shirt as she was covered in sweat.

"Hello?" she called as she entered the garden. Then Lauren smelled her. It was the Born woman. Her scent made Lauren's whole body tremble.

The woman was bending down pulling insects off a flower stem. She turned to Lauren and smiled, standing back up. She was shorter than Lauren by at least a foot. Short, dark hair; swarthy skinned. She didn't appear to be Chinese, though she looked oddly familiar, like Lauren was seeing herself only older—maybe in her mid-thirties?

"Hello, my daughter. I have been waiting for you to come." The woman held out a hand for Lauren to take.

Lauren was more than a little stunned, but she took the woman's hand, and the woman pulled her closer.

The woman was very strong, her hands callused. She smelled Lauren's hand like Rami had when they first met. "How do you come to have two selves?" she asked, looking confused.

"I...uh...there was an accident and a Made bled into me," Lauren stuttered.

"Ah, that explains it." She let go of Lauren's hand. "It is fading. Your true self will purge it soon enough. These things take time. I have seen it before," she said.

"It is funny." She laughed. "There is very little I have not seen before. But you, you are new to me. I have not seen one so strong and potent in so very long."

"Who—who are you?" I asked.

Another voice at the opposite end of the garden answered. "Do not be an idiot, Lauren. She is Eve. She is the First."

"There you are. I wondered when you would show yourself," "Eve" said, turning in the direction of the voice.

A woman stood up from her hiding place behind a row of tall flowers. She was in all black tactical gear, had a silenced pistol in one hand, a couple grenades on her belt, and a small pack.

"You! You are Su," Lauren said.

Eve cocked her head, smelling the air. "Your true self is faded. How many generations, four or five?" she asked Su.

Su looked confused for a moment. "What? I do not know; at least three before me, maybe more. That is why I am here," she said, walking slowly forward, her pistol aimed at Lauren.

"I would have been happy to have Lauren's blood. But if you are here then I will take yours instead."

Eve smiled. "Mine? It is yours if you want it. But I warn you, living this long is a curse and a terrible burden," she said, spreading her hands apart.

"What? No, you cannot give it to her!" Lauren shouted.

"Sure, she can. And you're going to take it from her and give it to me." Su laughed. "Give it to me, and quickly, and I will let you live. Otherwise, I will kill you both and take it." She unslung her pack and tossed it one-handed to Lauren.

Lauren was fuming, but she didn't think she could get close enough to try to disarm her. She unzipped the bag. Inside was a clear plastic container.

"It's an intraosseous device," Su said.

"I know what it is," Lauren said tersely, "and I know how to use it. They had us practice in basic training to start IVs in a bone while we tended to the wounded on the battlefield."

"You, over there—sit on the bench. Roll up your pant leg." Su waved her gun at Eve.

Eve sighed and smiled as she sat down and rolled up her pant leg. "It's all right, Lauren, go ahead."

Lauren looked around but there were not any guards in sight and no monks either. Su shot the ground next to her, making her jump.

"Hurry up there, my window of success is closing and if it does you are both dead."

Lauren opened the case and checked the supplies. "Bitch," she muttered.

"Implant the hep-lock, inject ten ccs of sterile water, and draw the syringe back immediately. When it stops filling, cap it. No, better yet, put that fat needle on the end," Su said with a smug smile.

Lauren cleaned the shin, took the drill, and said, "I am sorry, but this is going to hurt. I had two of these put in my legs before."

"It is all right." Eve patted her shoulder. "It can't be worse than doing Yhin's special katas or birthing more babies than I can count."

Lauren pushed the needle against her shin and the drill quickly bored a hole into the bone, leaving a hep-lock port in place. Eve didn't even wince.

"Okay, that seems right." Lauren cleaned the hep-lock with an alcohol swab and attached the syringe, then slowly injected the water and drew it back.

"I've got eight ccs," she said.

"Good. That will do. Put the needle on it, then bring it here," Su demanded.

"Don't do anything stupid. We are almost done," she said as Lauren stopped a few feet in front of her.

"Now what?" Lauren asked.

"Inject it into my thigh. My journey out will be long. I want to keep it safe and viable," she said as she put her gun to Lauren's forehead. "Hurry up. *Ticktock.* The window is closing."

Lauren jammed the fucking thing into Su's leg hard, making sure it hit the bone. Then she pushed the marrow in.

"Huh. You are good at this," Su said with a sneer. "Maybe you should go into medicine." Then she pushed Lauren away from her, still holding the gun to her forehead. The syringe was still in her leg, but she pulled it free and let it drop to the ground, rubbing the sore spot with her hand for a few moments.

"All right, thank you both. My ride is coming." She began backing up toward the garden wall, keeping both Lauren and Eve covered with her gun. Then she grinned and shot Lauren in the leg. "Tit for tat, Lauren, tit for tat."

Lauren shouted in anger as she fell to the ground, holding her wounded leg. "Fucking bitch!"

Eve flicked her wrist and a steel spike appeared, getting stuck in the end of Su's gun and nearly knocking it out of her hand. Then she rushed to Lauren's side with another spike in hand from up her sleeve.

A large black drone with silenced rotors came over the wall and hovered above Su's raised hand. She flung her disabled gun aside and reached out for one of the grenades while grabbing the drone's handle with her other hand. It took off slowly but quickly gained velocity.

"I may check in with you from time to time, Lauren. I think we could be friends someday. We will laugh about this over drinks!" She laughed as she disappeared over the bamboo forest.

"Fuck, my leg hurts," Lauren moaned. Eve helped her put pressure on it.

Then she heard Henri call out from the other entrance. "All clear! All clear. Lauren has been shot in the leg," he cried, rushing to her side.

Yhin's security force bolted through both entrances. One of the men was carrying a first aid kit.

"I cannot believe she got away with it. Where the hell were you guys?" Lauren shouted at them. She was hurting and so mad, and all she wanted to do was scream. "Why didn't you kill her?" she asked, turning to Eve.

Eve smiled and said, "I dislike killing. There was no need. She was disarmed and the poor foolish thing does not know it yet, but she is already dead."

"We could not risk rescue until she was clear," Commander Yi said loudly, walking up beside them and interrupting the discussion. "You did well, Lauren. Your being shot was not part of the plan, though. I am sorry."

"Wait, what? Are you kidding me? *This* was a plan?" Lauren hissed through clenched teeth.

The med tech who was examining me was being rough with my leg.

"It is through and through not bleeding much. You should be okay once I get it patched up," he said.

"Actually, it was Henri's plan. I made a few tweaks after discussing it with Yhin," Yi said ruefully.

"Your plan?" Lauren turned to Henri.

"Yes, I am so sorry, but the only way to catch her was to draw her out. We delayed getting here. Yi left her a few breadcrumbs of intel so that she would know this was where we were coming. He made a big show with that motorcade taking us to the private jet at the airport. She got here quicker than we thought, though."

Eve stood up. "And then I changed the plan, as I wanted to meet this woman, Su."

"My men will track her down now," said Yi. He walked off and began speaking into his phone in Mandarin. Eve followed him and they talked for a bit. Yi repeatedly shook his head until Eve asked for his phone and spoke into it. When she handed it back to him, Yi put the phone to his ear and nodded in agreement with whomever was on the other end of the line. Then he shrugged.

Eve walked back over to Lauren and Henri. "What was that about?" Henri asked.

"I told him he didn't need to track her down and to call off his men," she said, smiling.

"What? Why?" Henri was incredulous.

"As I said before, she is already dead; she just does not know it yet. If she is strong, she may live a few more hours or even make it until morning. But she will die in agony," she said, still smiling.

"I am not like you. Neither Born nor Made. I am different, something else entirely. An anomaly that managed to pass a few useful genes on to you. We are cousins at best. My blood is toxic to other humans. It cannot be used to make Another. It has been tried and all who did so died horribly. I might have told her had she asked."

Lauren wasn't sure if it was the pain meds the tech just shot her up with, but she started to laugh. Henri shook his head and laughed too. Then Eve joined in. They laughed for a long, long time.

Epilogue

What a whirlwind the last six months have been. Eve's name is really Sha'nia but she doesn't use it, hasn't since her "First Life." She has had so many names that it doesn't feel like hers anymore; she just wants me to call her mom. I finally gave in as she wouldn't stop calling me daughter. We look enough alike that no one questions it. When someone asks or comments that she looks too young to be my mom, she says she had me when she was fifteen. We laugh and laugh all the time.

Can you believe she has never had a daughter? Nope, not one. All boys the whole time. Some weird quirk of her physiology. Can you imagine ALL BOYS for twenty thousand years? I don't know how she managed to survive.

She left the monastery a month after Henri and me. After two hundred years of meditation and practicing katas, she decided she needed to walk the world again. She has missed so much since she left France after her last son died. She's lost a lot of sons and most too soon, she said. She doesn't think she will have any more kids—unless she meets the right man of course. That's okay, though; I'm not ready for a brother.

She invited me to go with her on her "world walk." We are currently in Henri's Winnebago driving out to the West Coast. I want her to meet my grandfather. I will tell him that she is a long-lost aunt on my mother's side and that I found her on Ancestry.com.

Eve never got to travel to the Americas, so we are going to do that for a bit. She'd also never been on a plane until she flew here. So many "never dids" for both of us. She told me that she cannot smell Kazim's blood in me anymore, so that's a relief.

She doesn't think she is fully human, a *Homo sapiens* at least, and speculates that she is another race altogether, like Neanderthal or Denisovan. Maybe she really is the first of a new line of humans. Who knows? Lately she's been reading a ton of anthropology books, a lot of which are way over my head. She has been alive since the ice that covered Europe and Asia started to melt.

I ask her lots of questions, like how does she still have her teeth? Wouldn't they have worn down or rotted by now? She just shakes her head every time I ask things like that.

Her answers are always something like: "I do not know. When one hurts really badly, I work it loose and pull it out and then a new one just grows back in."

Does she still get her period?

"Yes, I do but it is very light and only a few times a year now. It used to be much more often than that."

And how come she hasn't run out of eggs yet and can she still become pregnant?

"I do not know. It must be the same reason my teeth grow back. I think I can still have children, or at least I was still able to two hundred years ago. It took a long time to conceive the last few, so I think my body is finally slowing down in that regard."

When I asked her where the word Curvel came from, what it means, she laughed, "It is from my ancient people's language. It means little blood sucker."

It has been interesting learning about her many lives and travels.

I miss Henri more than a little. We finally scratched that itch, and my god was it worth it. We are not in love or anything, but the sex is awesome, and we genuinely care for each other. Who knows, maybe we will end up together, maybe not. He's a bit old for me, at least right now.

Besides, he may not ever get over the loss of his wife, no matter how long he lives. For some people there is only one love, and it is forever. I think that is just who he is.

He's in Quebec rebuilding his house, by himself. All by hand like he did the first time. His friend Jack was killed by Benton's men, and he feels pretty awful about it, but there wasn't anything we could do. He adopted Jack's dogs and animals and just needs time to work through the loss.

He sent me the remaining gold and silver from under the cistern to start my nest egg. If I am going to live a long time, I need to start thinking about the wonders of investing and compound interest. Rami helped me set up a trust and a portfolio. Yhin gifted me $1.2 million as a reward for what we did to restore the Circle and protect the Ring. He assured me he would move heaven and earth if I needed help with anything.

Mom is set up already with more money than I think she could spend even if she lived another twenty thousand years. I will have to plan to die in twenty or so years and start over as someone new, someplace new.

Yhin reconstituted the Circle, which seems to be going well. At least as far as I can tell. I don't really like politics. But I have to say, I've liked everyone in the Circle and the Ring that I've met so far.

Rami is training a new batch of emissaries. He seems happy and has a new girlfriend named Esther, one of the other Made in the office. She is one of the women who warned me off the Spanish guy. Esther is Italian, with a fiery temper, and is a little older than Rami. She keeps him on his toes. They both seem happy.

I think about that Spanish guy occasionally. He is so fine.

I kidnapped Napoleon. He is my good boy now. I may get him a girlfriend when we go back to Maine. He deserves love too.

Mom is teaching me Mandarin; then we'll move on to strengthen my French. Oh, and kung fu too! That has been a revelation, and challenging, but also a lot of fun.

I think I am finally getting past what happened with my parents and what I went through in Afghanistan. Right now, I just want to see the world and enjoy as much as I can. I don't know how long I have. But then, none of us do.'

Turn the page for a sneak peek at the thrilling sequel to Ageless:

The Wolf

Bonus – Chapter One

Flensburg, Germany, 1908

"Gero! What are you doing in my study?" Wilhem called through the open door. He was a tall man, with wide shoulders and narrow hips. His fair hair was cropped short with a touch of gray at the temples. One could not miss the obvious Norwegian ancestry with those pale blue eyes set deep above high cheekbones.

"Playing with my men, Papa," Gero answered, his small voice echoing from the large room.

The study had high ceilings and walls filled with books. A large diorama on a table depicting the Battle of Waterloo filled the center of the space. Displays of various weapons and armor going back centuries stood between the bookcases.

"Gero." Wilhelm's voice hardened as he strode into the room.

"I've told you before not to touch my... Oh." He found Gero sitting on the floor behind the diorama with his blocks and tin soldiers in lines facing each other.

"This looks very good. Which battle is it?" Wilhelm's face and voice softened.

Gero looked at his father, beaming. His hair was pale yellow, and his eyes were just as blue as his father's.

"It is the war of the cabbages. These men like green cabbage, and these men like purple, and they are fighting over which one is better," he said confidently, repositioning two of his men.

Wilhelm sat down on the floor next to his son.

"I see. A very serious battle then. Who do you suppose will be victorious?"

"I don't know yet. I think they are evenly matched."

Gero was holding a small wooden figure, a man wearing a wolfskin cape, with a spear in one hand and a large shield in the other. His eyes were wide, and he was biting the top of his shield. One of Odin's berserkers.

"Ah, I see you've not placed all your men on the field," Wilhelm remarked. "That one looks very powerful. He could tip the battle either way. Which side is he on? They will surely win."

"Leif doesn't like cabbage," Gero said, shaking his head.

Wilhelm smiled and nodded in agreement.

"I don't like it either."

"Will you tell me the story of Leif again?" Gero asked.

Wilhelm's eyes twinkled. "Yes, of course." He began to move Gero's men around.

"It was a long time ago, nearly one thousand years. Leif the Younger was the greatest warrior from our tribe. He was a worshiper of the great god Odin, long before we came under the Christian god's grace. He and his men were the Ulfheonar. They dressed in wolfskins, and they wielded axes and spears and carried mighty shields into battle. A great war had started when King Harold the Fair Hair was consolidating all the tribes into one kingdom. A usurper rose up among the ranks of the tribes that refused to join him. A terrible battle ensued at Hafrsfjord when they clashed."

He continued to move Gero's men around.

"Here was the line. There were two thousand men in defensive positions along the river. Here King Harold had five hundred, and another five hundred were here. The king was on the offensive against a superior force, and it looked as though he could not prevail against such a much larger, well-fortified enemy force.

"Leif the Younger arrived with his Ulfheonar. They were two hundred of his best men, and Leif offered their service to the king."

Wilhelm placed the wooden figure of Leif on the field.

Gero's eyes grew wide as he listened.

"Leif and his men prepared for battle with a prayer to Odin. Then they rushed the defenses in a tight group. They howled like wolves, beating and biting their shields as they ran. The defenders trembled in fear and shrank back as the berserkers struck their line. Their spears bit deep; axes cleaved heads with every stroke. They killed five hundred in that attack and broke the enemy's line. The king's army rushed in from the two flanks." He moved the men around again.

"So powerful was Lief's attack that they penctrated all the way to the usurper's guard." He grabbed an ornate silver spear from the display and thrust it into the air.

"He thrust his spear through the man's chest, pinning the usurper to the palisade wall, and then chopped off his head with a blow from his axe, which broke the will of the defenders. The king's men routed the rest."

Gero's mouth hung open in awe. Wilhelm replaced the spear and took down a silver wolf mask, holding it for Gero to look at.

"Many songs were sung extolling Leif's legendary deeds. The king rewarded him with this silver mask and spear, which were passed down through the ages to me. It will be yours when I pass, and you in turn will tell your sons of their ancestors' great deeds." He placed the mask over Gero's face. Gero held it tight with his small hands and howled like a wolf.

"Arooooo!" he cried. "Aroooo!"

About the Author

Jon Lewis

Jon Lewis grew up in Maine and joined the USAF right out of high school, where he served as an avionics technician and had the good fortune to travel all over the world. After that, he returned to school to become a respiratory therapist. After he graduated, he and his wife returned to Maine to raise their children. He had a very satisfying career caring for his fellow veterans and has now retired from healthcare to pursue his lifelong dream of becoming a published author. He now lives in a small coastal town with his beloved wife, Niki, spending his time traveling, writing poetry and short stories, and watching his seventh grandchild grow up.

Printed in Great Britain
by Amazon